The Long Road Home

Devil Chaser's MC

by
L. Wilder

The Long Road Home

Devil Chaser's MC Romance Series

Copyright 2016 L. Wilder

All rights reserved.

Cover Model: Colin Wayne
www.facebook.com/colinwayneofficial

Photographer: Michael Stokes
michaelstokes.net

Cover Design: Robin with Wicked By Design
www.wickedbydesigncovers.com

Editing & Formatting: Daryl Banner
www.darylbanner.com

Book Teasers: Neringa Neringiukas

Personal Assistant: Amanda Faulkner PA
www.facebook.com/amanda.faulkner.1023

Table of Contents

Dedication

For all of you who need your happy ending.

May you find yours this holiday season.

Prologue

The season had officially turned. Fall was making her presence known in the quaint, little lake town of Paris, Tennessee, and Sunny couldn't have been happier. She loved the fact that the leaves were changing into beautiful golden yellows and brightly colored oranges. The evening air had turned cool and crisp as it whipped around, making the leaves dance at her feet. She looked up when she heard the familiar sounds of geese honking back and forth as they migrated to their secret coves across the lake. It was her favorite time of year, and she was tickled that it was downright chilly as she picked up the last of the empty beer bottles from the tables. Being the lead waitress at Hidden Creek, it was Sunny's job to make sure that everything was cleaned up before closing. It wasn't exactly the best part of her job, but it had to be done.

She was almost finished clearing off the back deck when Casey, one of the other waitresses, peeked her head out the back door and asked, "Do you need any help?"

"Nope. I got it."

"Cool. Then, I'm going to start on the bathrooms." The door clicked shut as Casey tromped down the stairs.

"Have at it, chick," she chuckled.

Sunny stopped for a moment and ran her hands quickly up and down her arms, trying to stir up a little warmth in her body. She couldn't help but smile when she thought about the bonfire she would be attending at Jaclyn's house later that night. Every year, Jaclyn had a huge blowout for her birthday, and she invited everyone to come celebrate: friends, family, neighbors, and whomever she bumped into on the street. It was a tradition that Sunny had come to look forward to. In her mind, Jaclyn's party marked the day that she could officially pull out her fall wardrobe, including her tall, brown leather boots with the red piping down the back zipper. They were her favorite, and the fact that her best friend Katelyn wanted them more than life itself made her love them even more. For the party, she'd planned to wear those fabulous boots with one of her trademark t-shirts—the black one with the bear claw on the shoulder that said "What doesn't kill you will make you STRONGER – except for bears. Bears *will kill* you."

Once she was done cleaning up, she went downstairs and found Casey mopping the floor. "Since it's been so slow tonight, I was able to finish up both

2

bathrooms. Once I'm done with this, I'll get ready to close out my register."

"Awesome. You can head on out as soon as you're finished."

"You sure?"

"Yep. I'll get the trash out and that should just about do it for the night."

"Great. I'll see you over at Jaclyn's, right?"

"You know it, girl. I wouldn't miss it. I've been looking forward to this party for weeks now. I've just got a few more things to finish up here and then I'll be on my way."

Her boss, Dan, who was also a successful farmer, was busy picking corn. Since he couldn't be there, he had asked her to close for the night. It was nothing out of the norm; she'd closed the bar many times over the last year. But tonight she had all her friends waiting for her at the bonfire, so she was more than a little eager to get things wrapped up. Thankfully, the late night party season was over. The summer crowds had finally gone, and they were back to their local few who came by for a quick bite to eat or to pick up forgotten groceries. Since they weren't busy, Dan had given them the okay to close early. As soon as the last customer left, Casey and Sunny had hustled to get everything shut down for the night.

By the time Sunny had changed clothes and gotten the bar locked up, it was after ten. Casey had already

3

gone, leaving Sunny completely alone as she made her way out to her car. It was something she'd done hundreds of times before, but something about that night was different. From the moment she'd stepped onto the gravel of the parking lot, she'd gotten an uneasy feeling. As she walked towards her car, there was a loud clatter that echoed from the back of the bar. The uneasy feeling quickly turned to panic, stopping Sunny dead in her tracks. The tiny hairs on the back of her neck stood straight up as she slowly turned to look behind her.

There was something familiar about the anxious feeling she felt growing in the pit of her stomach. Over the last year, she'd felt it many times, more than she could even begin to count. It had all started when she broke things off with her longtime boyfriend. It turned out he wasn't the man she thought he was, not even close. There was a time when she'd liked Drew, maybe even loved him. He was so handsome and fun to be with, and he seemed to have his life together—a good job, a nice place to live, and a decent ride. Unfortunately, after many months of dating, things started to change. He became overly possessive to the point of insanity. He'd constantly ask where she'd been and who she'd been with and never seemed to trust her about anything. Eventually, she discovered why. He'd been screwing around with the girl next door. She immediately broke things off and sent him packing.

That's when everything went to hell.

Over the next few months, she had countless run-ins with him, from pleading phone calls that always turned menacing and hateful to unexpected visits that never failed to turn into some kind of heated argument, and letter after letter left in random places at various times throughout the day. She'd tried everything to get him to back off and leave her alone, but he just wouldn't let it go. When he'd taken things too far and grabbed her, breaking her wrist, she'd had enough.

It was then that she'd considered asking Bishop for help. He was the president of the Devil Chaser's MC and a close family friend. She knew if anyone could get Drew to stop harassing her, it would be Bishop, but just when she'd decided to go talk to him, Drew disappeared. There were no more phone calls. No more letters. No more unannounced visits. He was gone.

She couldn't see a thing through the blanket of darkness that surrounded the bar and woods behind it. Sunny knew there were all kinds of wild critters back there, from raccoons to possums, so she turned back, convincing herself that it was just some rodent searching for its dinner. Still feeling a little off, she lengthened her stride, rushing to her car as she dug into her purse and hunted frantically for her keys. Just as her fingers wrapped around the cold familiar metal chain, she heard, "Hey there, Sunshine. Where ya headed in such a rush?"

The Long Road Home

Her breath was ripped from her lungs as she listened to the familiar sound of her ex-boyfriend's voice. She had no idea where he'd come from. There was no sign of his truck in the empty parking lot, and she'd never even heard him walk up. Her heart raced with panic as she slowly turned to face him. He stood behind her with a beer in his hand and a sinister smile spread across his face. She silently berated herself for ever thinking that he was hot. The man was an arrogant asshole with a decent haircut. Nothing more. "What are you doing here, Drew? You shouldn't be here."

The gravel crunched beneath his boots as he took a step closer. She could smell the alcohol on his breath as he snarled, "And who's to say I shouldn't be here, darlin'? I don't see anyone here but you."

Fear washed over her as the reality of his words sank in. There was no one there to call out to for help. There was no one there to stop the psychotic stalking prick from hurting her once again, only now she was afraid he wouldn't stop at just a broken wrist. She did her best to swallow her panic as she took a step back, fumbling with her keys as she searched for the unlock button on her remote. "I don't have time for this, Drew. I'm already late."

He placed a hand on the driver's side door, blocking her only entrance to the car as he said, "Where you headed?"

She considered her answer, thinking maybe if she

was just cordial and talked to him for a minute, he'd let her go. But when she looked at his face and saw the glimmer of hate and anger in his eyes, she knew exactly what was in store for her. It didn't matter what she said. She knew he had come there for one reason and one reason only, so she answered, "I've got people expecting me, Drew. If I'm not there soon, they'll come looking for me."

"*They'll come looking for me*," he mocked. "We're twenty minutes away from the bonfire, thirty minutes or more from town, and there's not a soul in sight. Doesn't look like anyone is gonna be looking for you, Sunshine. At least, not for a while." She watched in terror as he took a long pull of his beer, making her wonder just how much he'd had to drink already. His eyes were locked on hers as he took another step towards her. "Looking good tonight, Sunshine. I'm sure you'll turn some heads wearing that."

Trying her best to rein in his anger, she answered, "It's just jeans and boots, Drew. It's not a big deal."

"Don't try to bullshit me. I know what's up."

His voice was deep and laced with rage as he spoke. Sunny glanced up at him, noting the pulsing veins thickening around his neck, and she knew without a doubt things were about to get bad.

"Really, it's just a bonfire."

"With a bunch of drunks pawing over what's mine."

Terror surged through her as he eased closer and placed his hand in her hair, flipping his thumb through the loose strands. Without warning, he twisted it around his knuckles, pulling her roughly over to him. She whimpered and cried as she tried to break free from his grasp, but it was pointless. She was no match for him. He leaned over her, and she could feel the heat of his breath at her neck as he said, "Nothing's changed, Sunshine. You're mine. You'll always be mine."

"You're hurting me!"

"And you didn't fucking hurt me?" he spat. "You don't think it felt like a goddamn knife in the back when you broke it off with me? I fucking loved you." His grip around her hair grew tighter as he yelled. The muscles in his body grew taut as his anger rose, and she knew there was little that she could do to stop him, but she had to try.

"Let me go!" With a quick, firm thrust, she lifted her knee between his legs, hitting him with such force that his own knees buckled. His beer splashed across her shirt as he loosened his hold on her hair. She quickly pulled away from him, but only managed to take a few steps before he grabbed her arm and yanked her back over to him. He reared back and slammed his beer bottle against the side of her face. She cried out in pain as she felt the bones in her jaw break with the force of the hit. Her hands immediately wrapped around her head as she tried to shield herself from the continuous blows, but it was useless. There was nothing she could do to protect herself from his wrath. One hit after another pummeled her tiny body until she fell limp to the ground. When his boot slammed into her side, she wondered how much more she could take. There was no doubt in her mind that he would kill her, and at that moment, she didn't care. She just wanted it to be over. Thankfully, after one brutal kick to her head, it was. Everything around her went black.

Chapter 1

It was just before twelve when Bishop left his office and headed out to the garage to find Bull. He wanted to catch him before he broke for lunch. He'd just gotten a call about a 1967 Chevy truck and a 1970 Chevy Nova that needed to be picked up in Kentucky. The owner wanted them both fully restored by Thanksgiving, so he made arrangements for Bull and Otis to pick them up later that afternoon. Since they didn't have any time to waste, he wanted the guys to start breaking them down first thing the following morning. As Bishop had always hoped, the club's restoration business had continued to grow. Over the past year, they'd updated all their equipment so they could get the work done in less time. The brothers had always been good, but with the new expansion, they'd been able to take things to another level. Word had gotten out that they were the best, and people from all over the Mid-South turned to them for both classic car and bike restorations. Bishop's dream had become a reality, and financially, the club was doing better than ever.

He felt a sense of pride as he walked into the

10

garage, seeing his guys busy working on their different projects. Sheppard was putting the final touches on the 1960 Chevy pickup he'd found for Goliath. He'd come across it on his way home from the club, and knowing that Goliath was looking for a pickup for Lily, he thought he might be interested in restoring it. After just one look, Goliath was hooked, and by the following day, the old, beaten-up pickup was sitting in the club's garage. After a few long months of work and a fresh coat of cherry red paint, they'd managed to bring her back to life. She was a real beauty, and there was no doubt Lily was going to love it.

Bishop walked over to the truck and ran his hand over his salt and pepper beard as he checked out their progress. He nodded with approval. "She's really coming along."

Sheppard took an old rag off the hood and wiped his hands, trying his best to get rid of some of the dirt and grime. "Yeah, she's looking great, but she's still missing a little at start up."

"Too bad Renegade's not here to have a look at it."

"Yeah, he'd know what to do, but they aren't going to be back from their honeymoon for another week. We can't wait that long. Goliath's planning to give it to Lily this weekend for her birthday."

"Then you're under the gun. Maybe it's just a bad coil or something."

"That's what we were thinking. Goliath went to the

back to get a new one. We'll see if that will do the trick."

"Hopefully that will do it."

"It better. Goliath is gonna lose his shit if we don't get this thing finished on time."

"He'll get it done. He always does." Bishop looked around the garage, and then asked, "You seen Bull?"

"Yeah, he's out back with Gavin. He stripped one of the bolts or something when he tried to put on his new exhaust, so Gavin's trying to fix it for him."

"Sounds about right. I've got some things to take care of, but let me know if you need me to take a look at it later."

"Will do."

Bishop headed to the back of the garage and found Gavin, one of the club's prospects, kneeling at the back of Bull's bike. After doing his time as a hang-around, Gavin had started prospecting. Over the past year, he'd proven to be a great asset to the club, in more ways than Bishop had expected. Not only was he good with his hands, but he was also good at paying attention. He never failed to go above and beyond anything he was asked to do, and Bishop knew it wouldn't be long before he'd officially earn his patch into the club.

"Bull," Bishop called. Bull's attention was immediately drawn away from the work Gavin was doing on his bike. "Gonna need you and Otis to make a run to Kentucky this afternoon."

"Sure thing. Where we headed?"

"Over to London. Should be able to get there and back by tonight."

"No problem. I'll go round up Otis."

"Here are the directions. There'll be two cars, so take the thirty-five foot trailer."

Bull took the paper and shoved it into his back pocket. "We'll get it taken care of."

"Knew you would."

Once he was gone, Bishop peered over Gavin's shoulder, noting the large shorty exhaust that he was installing. "Damn."

Gavin smiled. "Yeah, we'll be hearing him from miles away with these things."

"We'll have to keep his ass in the back of the line from here on out."

"No doubt about that." Gavin took a step back, admiring his work. "But you know what they say about chrome… *It won't get you home, but it might get you laid*."

"Shit." Bishop chuckled as he turned and started back towards the clubhouse. "Got some things to take care of in town. Let me know if you need anything."

"Will do."

As Bishop headed back into the clubhouse, his mind was bombarded with all the things he needed to get done and how little time he had to do it. Things were piling up, but he tried to think of it as a good sign. Busy meant money, and lots of it.

On his way to his bike, he walked through the bar. He thought the room was empty until he spotted Sunny sitting quietly over in the corner. She had several books sprawled out across two of the tables, and she seemed completely focused on her work as she typed away on her laptop. He stopped for a moment to look at her, remembering how she had looked only a year ago. It did him good to see her trudging away at her school work. After quitting her job at Hidden Creek, she'd started taking classes at the local community college and had made plans to attend one of the state schools in the spring. He'd done everything in his power to help her, and she'd been making real strides in getting her life back together. He couldn't have been more pleased to see her doing so well after all she'd been through.

As a kid, she'd always had a smile on her face and a *knock-'em-dead* attitude, and it meant a lot to him that she was good to Wyatt whenever he was over at her mother's place. She was a sweet kid, and for a long time, he'd worried she'd never get past the night she was attacked. When Glenda, Sunny's mother, had called that night to ask Bishop and the brothers to check on her, he had no idea what they'd find when they pulled into the parking lot of Hidden Creek. He sure as hell hadn't expected to find Sunny lying face down on the gravel, unconscious and fighting for her next breath. With all the swelling and blood-soaked clothes, she'd been almost unrecognizable.

It had taken several surgeries, months in the hospital, and hours upon hours of physical therapy for her to get better—*physically*. Mentally was a different story. After all these months, she'd never really healed all that was broken inside her. The nightmares and panic attacks were slowly dying down, but she had yet to remember everything that had happened. There were a lot of unanswered questions, and while he knew the answers to some of them, he prayed that she never would. The brothers had done what they could to help her, and since the moment they'd found her lying helpless on the ground, she'd been under their protection. They'd cleaned up the mess and dealt with the cops, doing whatever they could to erase what had happened. Some things were just better left forgotten, and that night was one of them.

Even though she tried to hide it, he could still see the pain lurking behind her eyes. Everyone who knew her could see it. She was still fighting her inner demons, but he hoped that her focus on college and getting her degree might help her move on. For the most part, it had been working. She'd started venturing out on her own and stopped hiding in her room for days on end, and had even started going out with the girls. She didn't stay out long, but it was a start. That positive attitude of hers was trying to fight its way back, doing what it could to win out over the dark that was raging inside of her. Bishop felt certain that in time, it would, and he was willing to stand in the gap until that day.

Remembering how much he had to do, he turned to leave. Just before he walked out, the front door flew open. Seconds later, John Warren came charging inside with Lily and Grace following close behind.

"JW!" Lily called out to him to no avail.

He kept running until he slammed into Bishop, wrapping his arms around his legs as he said, "Hey, Bishop!"

Bishop knelt down and lifted him into his arms. "Hey, little man. Where you headed off to in such a hurry?"

"I wanna tell Daddy about the lizard I found in da garage."

After Lily's sister was killed, Lily came to Tennessee in hopes of protecting her nephew from the same fate. She met Goliath while working in the bar, and it didn't take long for sparks to fly. They fell for each other and decided they wanted to be a family. After several long, agonizing months and lots of questions about JW's paternity, they finally managed to adopt JW. Since then, they'd had their own child, Grace, who was about to turn one. They'd both gotten the family they'd always wanted and more.

Bishop lowered JW to the ground and smiled when he looked up at him with those inquisitive dark green eyes. "He's out working in the garage, but he'll be done soon."

He turned and looked at his mother. "Momma, can I go out to da garage?"

"No, JW. You know you can't go out there when Daddy's working. You can tell him all about your lizard when he's done."

His bottom lip rolled out into a pout, but it faded quickly when he spotted Sunny sitting over in the corner. He raced over to her, nearly knocking her out of her seat when he crawled into her lap. Excitedly, he started telling her all the details of his great catch.

Lily walked over to the bar counter and reached for Grace's highchair. Once she had her settled, she turned to Bishop and asked, "You gonna tell me why I can't go out to the garage? Every time I try to go out there, one of the guys finds some excuse for me to not go in. I know something's up."

"No idea what you're talking about."

She rolled her eyes and let out an exaggerated sigh. "Somehow I doubt that. You always know exactly what's going on around here."

A sly smile spread across his face. "Maybe so, but that doesn't mean I'm going to tell you."

"Didn't figure you would."

Lily turned her attention back to Grace and placed several crackers on the tray of her highchair. Just as she took her sippy cup out of the diaper bag, Goliath and Sheppard walked in with Gavin following close behind.

Goliath headed over to Lily and gave her a light kiss on her temple. "Got any plans for lunch?"

"We ate before we came. I've got to check the inventory and stock the coolers before I put the kids down for their nap. Want me to run to the kitchen and make you guys some sandwiches or something?"

"No need for that, sweetheart. You've got your hands full. Besides, I need to make a run into town, so we'll grab a burger while we're there."

There was a loud commotion behind them, drawing their attention over to Sunny and John Warren. Her books were now scattered all over the floor along with several of her papers. Lily started over towards her to help, but Gavin beat her to the punch. He'd already started gathering Sunny's things and placing them back on the table.

"I'm sorry," JW pouted. "It was an accident."

"It's okay, sweetie," Sunny assured him. "We'll get it all picked up."

Sunny quickly joined Gavin on the floor and helped him gather the rest of her things. Once they were done, Gavin stood up and winked at John Warren. "There ya go, bud. Got it all picked up."

Sunny stood up and smiled as she said, "Bet your dad will want to hear about that lizard you caught."

His eyes filled with excitement as he turned and rushed over to Goliath, shouting, "Hey, Daddy! I caught a lizard today!"

Once he'd gone, Sunny looked over to Gavin and said, "Thanks."

He gave her a slight nod, then turned and walked back over to the guys. It was one of his typical moves with Sunny. Whenever she was around, the self-assured, tough guy faded away and he became quiet and subdued. He wasn't very good at hiding that he had a thing for her. Everyone knew it except for Sunny. She thought he didn't like her, mainly because he acted so differently than the other guys. While the other brothers would talk and cut up with her, Gavin kept his distance. She figured he thought she was some kind of idiot or trailer trash for getting tangled up with the wrong guy, but that wasn't true—not even close.

When Gavin made it back over to the bar, Sheppard gave him a smirk and said, "You ready to go, Prince Charming?"

"I'm set."

"Got some parts that need to be picked up in McKenzie. After lunch, I'm gonna need you to go pick 'em up."

"No problem."

As they started for the door, Gavin glanced back over to where Sunny was sitting. She'd started back to work on her paper and didn't notice him staring.

Gavin knew he hadn't earned the right to pursue her. He was still prospecting, and Sunny was considered Bishop's family. He'd have to wait for his approval before he made his intentions clear to her, but he could be patient. He just hoped that she would be able to see through his past and to the man he'd become, something he had never been able to do himself. The choices he'd made were always present and right in his face every time he saw his son, John Warren. Even though he knew he'd made the right decision where his child was concerned, he doubted any woman would ever really understand why he'd done it. Still, that didn't stop him from thinking about his future—the future he wanted with the girl who taunted him in his dreams. The girl who filled the world's darkness with light, just like her name: Sunny.

Chapter 2

Gavin had his reasons for moving to Tennessee, mainly because he'd had suspicions that John Warren might have been his child. He needed to see for himself that he was okay, so he packed his bags and started prospecting for the Devil Chaser's. It didn't take him long to see that his new brothers were good men. Family came first, and Goliath was no different. Time and time again, he made it clear that he would do anything for Lily and JW. He loved them and bent over backward to make sure they were happy. John Warren wasn't his blood, but that never mattered to him. In his eyes, he was his son.

By the time the paternity test proved that he was John Warren's father, Gavin knew there was no way he could ever take him away from Lily and Goliath. He could see that JW was happy, truly happy, and it was clear to see how much they loved him. John Warren had found his home with them, and Gavin loved him too much to disrupt his little world. That didn't mean Gavin wouldn't be a part of his life, and thankfully, Goliath and Lily wanted it that way. He spent time with JW at the club, and Lily often invited him over just so they could be together. In fact, today she'd called to tell him that Goliath could use some help putting together JW's new swing set. He didn't hesitate going over to give him a hand.

They spent most of the afternoon piecing it all together, and once it was done, Goliath turned to him and said, "Never thought we'd get this damn thing put up."

"It's awesome. He's gonna love it."

He'd barely gotten the words out of his mouth when the back door flew open and John Warren rushed out. "I wanna swing!"

Goliath smiled. "Come on, buddy. Try it out."

JW raced over to him and threw his hands up. "Up!" Goliath reached down and lifted the boy into the swing, giving him a light push. "More, Daddy!"

Gavin watched them together and couldn't help but smile. As a kid, he'd never really spent a lot of time with his father, and he was glad John Warren had Goliath. He was a good man, a good friend, and an even better father. After an hour of playing, John Warren started to tucker out. Goliath picked him up and said, "Time for your bath and bed, little man."

"But, I not done."

"You are for now."

When they started for the door, Gavin told them, "I'm gonna head out. Y'all have a good night."

"Thanks for your help, brother. I'll see you at the garage in the morning."

Once he was gone, Goliath took John Warren

inside. Lily fed him his dinner, and then put him in the tub for his bath. Goliath was rocking Grace in his recliner when he called out to her. "I think we should call Maverick to come down. He'll want to be here when Gavin gets his patch."

Lily walked into the living room with JW in her arms and sat down on the sofa as she towel-dried her son's hair.

"When do you think y'all will do it?"

"Figure it will be in a couple of weeks. His year is almost up."

She looked over at her husband with their daughter in his arms, noting how small she looked curled up against her father's muscular chest, and even though she'd seen them like that hundreds of times, she was still in complete awe of how sweet they looked together. "I think that would be great. And if she's up to it, tell Maverick to bring Henley and the baby, too."

"You okay with them staying here?"

"Yeah! I think that'd be great. I'll get the guest room ready for them."

"Ready? What's to get ready? No one's stayed in there since we got the place done."

Before Grace was born they'd completely remodeled their home, gutting the kitchen and all the bathrooms and adding two additional bedrooms to the back of the house. Goliath had tried to convince Lily to buy a new place out closer to the lake, but she'd refused. Every time he had taken her to see a new place, she'd found some reason she didn't like it. He'd tried for months but never had any luck finding something that would convince her to move. She loved their small home. It was where she'd first fallen in love with Goliath, and she cherished all the memories they'd shared there, including the day that Maverick had brought their son home. So many good things had happened in that small house, and she just couldn't bring herself to leave. Seeing that she had her heart set on staying, Goliath got to work on fixing the place up. He'd done what he could on his own, and then hired a construction crew to do the rest. It had taken them some time, but they finally had the home they'd both always wanted.

"I need to wash the sheets and make sure everything is clean."

"Like I said, no one's been in there since we finished it."

"Goliath... just let me do my thing, and you do yours."

He rested his head on the back of the recliner and closed his eyes as he said, "Got no problem with that."

JW looked over to his mother, and with a puzzled look on his face, he asked, "What is your ting, Momma?"

"I do lots of things, sweetie... like putting you to bed right now. It's getting late, mister."

"I don't wanna go to bed. Gracie isn't in bed yet."

"She will be as soon as Daddy puts her there."

"Why can't Daddy put me to bed?" He pouted.

Goliath looked over to his son, smiling when he saw his bottom lip poking out. "How 'bout I go put your sister in her crib while Momma gets you in your pajamas, and then I'll come back to get you."

A satisfied smile spread across JW's face. "Okay."

Goliath eased out of the recliner and headed down the hall to Grace's room. He carefully laid her down in the crib and silently chuckled to himself as she instantly sprawled out across the mattress just like Lily did in their bed. When he looked down at his daughter, he couldn't imagine loving her more. Just being close to her brought him such joy and peace that it made the craziness of the world seem nonexistent. Knowing that JW was waiting for him, he turned and walked back into the living room.

John Warren's eyes lit up when he saw Goliath approach the sofa. It was well past his bedtime, but it was obvious that he wasn't ready to settle down for the night. "Are you gonna tell me a story?"

Goliath leaned down, lifting him into his arms as he answered, "A short one and then it's off to sleep with you."

"The Goodnight book."

"I think we can manage that." As they started down the hall, he called out to Lily in a silly voice, "I'll be back."

"I'm sure you will, Terminator."

She shook her head and laughed as she reached for the TV remote, flipping through the channels until she found one of her old favorites. Then, she lay down on the sofa, resting her head on one of the throw pillows. She hadn't realized how tired she was until she felt herself being lifted into Goliath's arms. Still half-asleep, she rested her head on his chest as she wrapped her arms around his neck. Feeling the warmth of his body next to hers stirred something inside of her. As he carried her down the hall to their room, she nuzzled against him, kissing him lightly on the neck.

"I want you," she whispered.

He looked down at her, seeing that needful spark in her eyes, and replied, "You got me."

As he walked into their room, he eased the door shut with his foot and carried her over to the bed. She smiled and watched appraisingly as Goliath began to undress. A sexy smirk crossed his face as he tracked her eyes roaming over his bare chest. He chuckled silently to himself as she started to squirm beneath the covers. He lowered his jeans to the floor, leaving only his boxer briefs. She inhaled deeply as he slowly lowered himself onto the bed beside her. Lily curled into his side and trailed the tips of her fingers along the lines of his tattoos, then looked up at him and said, "You're a tease."

"Who said I was teasing? I have every intention of giving you what you want," he growled.

Without any further hesitation, his hands reached up and tangled in the back of her hair as he dropped his mouth to hers. As his tongue brushed against hers, she felt a surge of heat soar through her body. The passion of his touch consumed her, filling her with want. When she couldn't wait a moment longer, she lifted herself off the bed and straddled him. A growl of approval filled the room as he guided her over his erection, rocking her back and forth against his hard cock. She continued to grind into him as he slowly moved his hands to the hem of her t-shirt, pulling it over her head and exposing her bare breasts. He let out a deep breath as she took her breasts in her hands, squeezing them firmly as she tilted her hips forward. Her skin flushed red with desire as she felt Goliath's erection throbbing beneath her. A hiss escaped his lips when she reached down, slipping the tips of her fingers into his boxers. With one quick twist, he flipped her onto her back and settled between her legs.

Goliath made love to his wife, again and again, until she was completely satisfied and sound asleep in his arms. The next morning, they were still in the bed together when he called Maverick.

Lily listened as Goliath said, "Yeah, she's just gotta change the sheets, and then we'll be all set." There was a pause and then he continued, "I already told her that.

But you know how women are about stuff like that." Shaking her head, Lily threw the covers back and pulled herself out of the bed. Goliath continued to talk as he watched Lily get dressed. "Good. I'll plan on you being here. Just let me know if something changes."

Once the arrangements had been made, he took a hot shower and then helped Lily get the kids ready for breakfast. Once they were settled, he got on his bike and headed over to the garage. As he pulled through the gate, he spotted Gavin kneeling at Sunny's car. He pulled his bike up next to him and after killing the engine, he asked, "Whatcha got going there, Knuckles?"

Gavin's focus remained on Sunny's back tire as Goliath got off his bike and walked over to him. "Her tire was a little low, so I thought I'd check it out."

"She know what you're doin'?"

"Nah. She's in there working on her paper, and I didn't want to bother her."

"Um-hmm." Goliath remembered doing the same kind of thing when Lily first came to town. He was always trying to help her out, showing in his own way that he cared for her without actually saying the words. "I'm sure she'll appreciate it."

"Just trying to make sure she's safe when she's out on the road. Was thinking of asking Bobby to check out her security system."

"He'll give it a look. Just let him know."

"I'll talk to him when I finish this." He stood up,

lifting the tire off the axle and into his hands. "Y'all get Lily's truck up and running?"

"We've just about got it. A few finishing touches and she'll be set to go."

"You've outdone yourself with that one, brother. It's something else."

"Yeah, it's coming along. You need a hand with this?" Goliath offered.

"Thanks, but I've got it."

Goliath followed Gavin to the garage and set to work on finishing up Lily's truck. He hadn't been working long when Sheppard walked up. Tension rolled off him as he walked over to the hood of the truck and peered inside. "Got the coil replaced?"

Goliath didn't miss the bite in his tone and asked, "Something got your panties in a twist?"

With a frown on his face, Sheppard turned to his brother. "Ana's having a hard time with one of her patients, and she's taking it pretty hard."

"What's going on?"

"There was an accident the other night. A family was hit by a drunk driver and their youngest is pretty bad off. He's been in a coma for days, and she's worried they're going to lose him. She's always had a soft spot where kids are concerned, and I'm not sure how she's going to handle losing this one."

"And you want to fix it for her, but you can't."

"Well, yeah. That's my job. When my girl has a

problem, I do what I can to make it right."

"Not much you can do about this, brother. You just gotta be there to listen."

Shep sighed with understanding. He leaned under the hood of the truck, checking all the plugs and the new coil. "Let's start her up."

Goliath opened the driver's side door and got inside. As soon as he turned the key in the ignition, she fired up and purred like a kitten. "Sounding good. Let's take her out on the road and test her out."

He closed the hood as he walked over and got inside the truck. Seconds later, Gavin watched as they pulled through the gate. He'd just finished putting a new tire on Sunny's car and was about to go get started on the new order that Bull and Otis had brought in, but he stopped cold when Sunny came rushing out the back door. Her hands were loaded down with books and her laptop, and she was obviously in a hurry as she scurried towards her car.

She kept walking, but suddenly stopped when she spotted Gavin standing by her car with a jack in his hand. While they never really talked, he didn't feel like a stranger to her. He was just one of the brothers, but that didn't keep the butterflies from dancing in the pit of her stomach whenever he was around. She told herself that it was just her nerves, and that it had nothing to do with how extremely handsome he was, but deep down she knew exactly why those butterflies were there. Her eyes slowly raised from his broad chest to his piercing gaze. "Uh… what are you doing?"

Over the past few months, she'd become accustomed to Gavin and all his little projects. There was always something he was working on: a rattle in her engine, a flickering light in her hallway, or a leaking faucet in the bathroom. The list was endless. She thought he'd done it all because he was ordered to, assuming that prospects just did that sort of thing, but Gavin had done it all on his own.

"Tire was low." A tingle crept down her spine as she noticed an intensity in his eyes that she wasn't expecting. She couldn't understand why he was always so quiet, and she wanted desperately to know what was going on in his mind, but he wasn't giving anything away. Finally, she let out a sigh and turned her attention back to the tire. "I wanted to make sure it was safe for you to drive."

"So, it's all good now? I can drive it?"

"Yeah. You're good to go." He walked over and took some of the books from her hands, helping silently as she opened her car door. Once she was seated inside, he asked, "You got your tagalong?"

She and Bishop felt better knowing there was someone keeping an eye on her so that Sunny didn't go anywhere without one of the prospects following. "Yeah, Conner is coming."

He carefully handed her each of her books. Just as

he was about to close her door, she looked up at him and said, "Thanks for the tire, Gavin."

With a slight nod, he eased the door shut and turned for the garage. She watched with wonder as he walked out of her line of sight. There was something about him that got to her, but she knew it didn't matter. She was still dealing with her own demons, and the last thing she needed was to take on his. Even with all the things she'd gone through over the past two years, there was no denying that she was attracted to him. No girl in her right mind could ignore those gorgeous, dark-green eyes and that ruggedly handsome face. It didn't help matters that he was built like some kind of Adonis and wore tight-fitting t-shirts that showed off his rippling muscles. She cursed herself anytime she caught herself fantasizing about him. She'd sworn off men, but she couldn't help but wonder what it would feel like to be wrapped in Gavin's protective arms and know that sense of security that she hadn't felt in so long. Trying to shake off her hormonal lapse, she pulled out of the lot and headed to class.

Later after class dismissed, she decided to go by the house and check on her mother. The last time they'd talked, her mom mentioned that she wasn't feeling well, so she wanted to go by to see if she was feeling any better.

When she got to the house, she found Myles and her brother, Tyler, sitting on the front porch swing next to her mom. With Conner waiting out by the curb, she got out of her car and walked over to them.

When she started up the steps, Tyler smiled proudly and said, "Hey, Sunny. Myles and I made the basketball team."

"That's awesome, dude." She leaned against the rail of the porch as she thought about the times they'd all played in her driveway. Tyler was always a great shot, and as he got older, he'd even managed to beat her— more times than she cared to admit. "They'd be crazy not to add you both to the team."

"Yeah, we're pretty awesome," Myles boasted. "Did you see that shot I made during tryouts, Ms. Glenda?"

"I did," Sunny's mother answered. "It was quite impressive."

Sunny could see that she was feeling well and smiled. "You doing better?"

"I am. I think it was just my allergies acting up. You know how the fall weather gets to me. How did you do on that English paper?"

"Good. Made an A. Now, I have two more to get done by Monday. It's going to be a long weekend."

"You could always come here for a few days. It might be quieter. Tyler is going to spend the night with Myles tomorrow night, so it'll just be me here."

"Maybe. I'll think about it."

Since she'd recovered from the attack, Sunny had

been staying at the clubhouse under club protection. Bishop and the guys had set her up in one of the empty rooms and made sure she had everything she needed to feel at home. She loved it there and no one blamed her, especially her mother. After everything that had happened with Drew, she knew her daughter felt safer under the watchful eye of Bishop and the boys. Being at the clubhouse gave her the sense of security she needed to move forward. Sunny was doing better, but that didn't mean her mother didn't worry. It was doubtful that there would ever come a time when she didn't. Her precious child had been through so much, and there was always the fear that her past would come crashing into her future. She just prayed that in time, her daughter would have the strength to face whatever came knocking at her door.

"You're always welcome, Honey. Just come and go as you like."

"Well, speaking of going, I'd better head out. I've got work to do." She walked over and gave her mother a quick hug before starting down the steps. As she got in her car, she turned to the boys and shouted, "Congrats on the team, guys. Proud of you."

Her mother wiped a tear from the corner of her eye as she watched Sunny pull out of the driveway. She loved her daughter, and her heart filled with pride seeing that she was doing so well. Life had thrown her some nasty punches, but she was still standing strong.

She had a long road ahead of her, and only time would tell if she'd be able to find her way home.

Chapter 3

Fall break had come and gone, and Thanksgiving was quickly approaching, bringing unpredictable weather along with it. Sunny was curled up in her bed studying for a big test when a bad storm rolled in. Lightning danced across the night sky, making the lights flicker above her head. There were some people who loved the loud rumble of thunder, but Sunny was not one of them – not in the least. In fact, she hated them. They freaked her out, especially when she was alone. A flash of lightning tore across her window, and she found herself counting silently to herself until she heard the loud roar of thunder. When it finally crashed outside of her window, she was *done*. She jumped out of bed and threw on a pair of jeans. While most of the guys had gone home for the night, she knew that Levi and Conner were around. She'd heard them talking earlier and knew they were pumped about playing some new video game that had just come out. Hoping that they hadn't changed their minds, she set out for the family room.

As soon as she opened her door, she could hear their shouts echoing down the hall as they cursed at each other over their game. She smiled and followed the sounds of their voices down the long hallway. When she walked into the room, she found them both sitting on the sofa, their elbows on their knees and controllers in their hands as they leaned towards the television. They were completely focused on their game, and neither of them seemed to notice as she walked over to the end of the sofa.

"You really suck at this. You know that, right?" Conner asked without looking at Levi.

"Fuck you. You suck."

If she didn't know better, she'd think they were both total gaming nerds with no life. But she'd seen them outside that room and knew without a doubt that they were far from nerds. They'd had a long stint in the military, and they'd both struggled to find a sense of peace since they'd returned. The games were just an outlet, giving them a way to forget they'd been to hell and back. They worked hard, spent hours on end in the garage and around the clubhouse doing what they could to help. She liked them, felt comfortable around them, and figured they'd be great company during the storm.

As she sat down next to Levi, he turned to her and smiled. "Hey there, Sunnybee. Want to play a round? Kick Conner's ass? It won't be hard. He sucks at this game."

Conner just shook his head. "Levi is the one who sucks. Just look at the damn score."

"I'll leave the ass kicking to you guys and just watch."

The lights flickered again, but neither of them

seemed to notice. She rested her head on the arm of the sofa and listened to them banter back and forth. It didn't take long for her to get her fill of the gaming world and their incessant shouting. When she stood to leave, Conner looked over and asked, "Where ya running off to?"

"I'm gonna go grab a snack and get back to studying. You guys have fun."

As she walked towards the door, Levi called out, "Holler if you need anything."

Trying her best to ignore the constant roll of thunder, she headed down the hall towards the kitchen. When she walked in, she found Gavin sitting at the table. Sunny smiled when she noticed he was eating her favorite: fruity kid's cereal with marshmallows—not exactly the kind she'd expect him to eat. To her, he seemed more like a hearty, corn flake kind of guy. She walked to the cabinet and got herself a bowl before she went over and sat down next to him. Gavin watched as she took the box in her hand and poured herself a large helping.

Just before she took her first bite, she said, "Pretty bad storm tonight."

"Cold front is coming in."

Those beautiful green eyes locked on hers, and she suddenly found it difficult to breathe. There was something about the way he looked at her, like she was the first drop of rain after a long, summer drought. The intensity in his eyes made her heart pound against her chest.

But then it was gone. His eyes dropped to his bowl of cereal as he scooped up his next bite. He continued to eat without saying a word, and Sunny quickly became frustrated. She just didn't get it. The other guys were so nice to her, always talking and cutting up with her, but Gavin was just the opposite. He would joke around and laugh with everyone else—just not her. He'd never said more than a couple of words to her, and it was really getting under her skin. She hated that she even cared. It shouldn't matter what he thought, but it did.

Just as Sunny worked herself into a tizzy, Gavin stood up from the table and took his empty bowl to the sink. Without saying a word, he started for the door.

Feeling angry and hurt, Sunny looked over at him and asked, "Why don't you like me?"

A puzzled look crossed his face as he turned towards her. "What?"

"*Why don't you like me*? It's a simple question. I just want to know."

He took a step towards her and crossed his arms. "What makes you think I don't like you?"

"It's pretty obvious, Gavin. You never have more than two words to say to me, and you get this weird look on your face whenever I walk into the room. I just want to know *why*."

He ran his hands over his face and sighed. "You've

got it all wrong, Sunny."

She leaned back against her chair. "Okay. So, tell me. How am I wrong? Explain it to me."

His jaw clenched tight as he stood there staring at her, contemplating what answer he could give that would explain his strange behavior, but nothing came to him. What could he say? There was no way in hell he could say how he felt about her. He couldn't tell her that he was completely captivated, that he was drawn to her for reasons he couldn't even begin to explain. Thankfully, the storm raging outside came to his rescue. With a loud and thunderous clap, the room plunged into darkness.

"Gavin?" Sunny shrieked as she shot up out of her chair.

Before she could call for him again, he was at her side. "I'm right here. I've got you."

She latched onto his arm, curling into him as another bolt of lightning flickered outside the kitchen window. Neither of them moved. Sunny's racing heart slowly began to calm under the protection of Gavin's hold. She felt safe with him, like nothing could harm her. Without releasing her grip, she asked, "Do you think the lights will come back on?"

"Maybe. The storm's getting pretty bad. I'll try to find a flashlight."

She wasn't ready to let him go, but she knew they couldn't just stand there in the dark. "I think there might be some candles and matches in the cabinet over the sink."

"I'll see what I can find. You stay put." Reluctantly, she loosened her hold. Relief washed over her when he said, "Found them."

Seconds later, the room filled with a soft, comforting glow. With a candle in his hand, he walked over to Sunny and asked, "You okay?"

"I'm fine. A little embarrassed for freaking out, but I'm okay."

He lifted his hand to the side of her face, gently tucking a loose strand of hair behind her ear. "No need to be embarrassed. Not with me."

She looked up at him, seeing that familiar look in his eye, and her breath caught in her throat. He was so close. His mouth was just inches away, and she couldn't help but imagine how his lips would feel pressed against her own. She was enchanted by him. Being so close to him made her forget about the hell she'd been through, all the sleepless nights and the heartache she'd felt for so long.

She relished the feeling and wanted to stay there in that moment, but fate had other plans. The lights flickered several times until they eventually came back on. Gavin took a step back and the moment was gone.

"I'll walk you back to your room."

Feeling more than a little disappointed, she followed him down the hall and to her door. She looked over to him, wishing that he wouldn't leave, and feigned a smile. "Thanks, Gavin."

She opened her door and as she stepped inside, Gavin said softly, "Sunny."

She turned to face him. "Yeah?"

His eyes were dark and intense as he stood there staring at her. Warmth washed over her as he continued. "I meant what I said. You were wrong. One day you'll see."

Before she could ask him what he meant, he turned and headed down the hallway. She wanted to call out to him, but she knew it was no use. If he wanted to tell her, he would have already done it. She closed the door and pulled off her jeans before crawling into bed. When she looked down at her phone, she saw that she'd missed several messages from Katelyn.

Katelyn:

Justin is an asshole. A complete and total asshole.

Katelyn:

I'm done with his sorry ass.

Katelyn:

"Out with friends"! Bullshit. What an asshole!

It was late, and Sunny figured her best friend had already gone to bed. But she still responded.

Sunny:

What's going on?

Seconds later, Katelyn replied.

Katelyn:

He told me that he was going riding with some of his stupid friends. He knew I couldn't go because of work. Asshole. Turns out he's been messing around with some chick named Kim.

Katelyn had always been a bit dramatic and never trusted any man—ever. She thought they were all lying, cheating assholes. Sunny couldn't blame her. They'd both had their share of rotten men, but Sunny really thought Justin was different.

Sunny:

Are you sure? I thought they were just friends or something.

Katelyn:

I'm sure. He took her to the damn mall. Guys don't go to the mall unless they want to get laid. Everyone knows that. But I'm over it. He can screw that stupid old cow all he wants.

The Long Road Home

Sunny:

I'm sorry. I really thought Justin was one of the good ones.

Katelyn:

Nope. He's a typical jerk. Just like all the rest.

Sunny:

There's a good guy out there. You'll find him.

Katelyn:

I'm about to give up all together. I'll be that cat lady out in some trailer by the lake.

Sunny:

Haha! That's not going to happen. Besides, you hate cats.

Katelyn:

I guess I better learn to like them, because they'll be all I've got.

Sunny:

It's late. Just forget about this for tonight and get some sleep.

Katelyn:

Wait. What about you? You doing okay?

Sunny:

I'm good. I've been studying.

Katelyn:

Well aren't you the party animal? Ha!

Sunny:

Don't you know it lol

Katelyn:

Let's meet up Tuesday after you get out of class.

Sunny:

Sounds good. Later Gator.

Sunny tossed her phone on her bed and picked up the book she had to read for her Lit class. She stared at the words on the page, but they all just blurred together. Her mind kept drifting back to Gavin, and the way she felt while wrapped in his arms. She liked it, more than she ever thought she could, and she wanted more. But the fear—the heart-pounding, earth-shattering fear—was holding her back. It haunted her day in and day out. She just couldn't get past it. There were days when it seemed to be getting better, but when she crawled into bed at night, the dreams would come. The nightmares would play out like a movie, only there were big chunks of time missing, making it impossible to remember everything that had happened that night. The memories were right there in the corner of her mind, but she couldn't reach them, no matter how hard she tried. She just hoped that in time the nightmares would stop, and she'd be able to move on. She'd accepted that she couldn't erase what had happened, and that it had changed her. Almost dying had made her realize just how fragile life was, and now she wanted to focus all of her energy on the future and its infinite possibilities.

Chapter 4

Gavin was sitting at the bar staring down at the black and white kitten he'd just bought for Sunny. He was just about to take it down to her room when he was suddenly overcome with doubt. Early today, as he'd driven by the animal shelter, the idea had popped into his head and he didn't stop to think it through. Now that the kitten was sitting in his lap, he started to wonder if Sunny even liked cats. He lifted the tiny kitten up to his face, looking her right in the eye as he asked himself, "What the hell was I thinking?"

She reached out her paw, placing it flat against his nose, and he quickly realized that her foot looked oddly large for an eight-week-old kitten. After closer inspection, he discovered that she had several extra toes—three of them on each paw. He groaned, thinking that he'd picked the one kitten that had something wrong with it. Berating himself for being such an idiot, he decided there was no way he could give it to Sunny—not now. He was just about to take it back to the pet store when Sunny walked into the bar. Her eyes widened with excitement when she spotted Gavin with the kitten in his hands. She rushed over to him and ran her hand over the kitten's head.

"Oh my goodness, that is the cutest kitten I've ever seen!"

"Yeah... well... umm." He watched as she took the cat from his hands and held it lovingly to her chest. "There's something wrong with its feet."

"What do you mean?" She took the kitten's paw in her hand and examined the extra toes. Her face lit up with curiosity as she said, "That is so wild! Where did you find her?"

Not ready to admit what he'd done, he turned and looked in the other direction. "She just wandered up. Found her out by my truck."

"Do you mind if I keep her?"

"She's all yours."

"Thanks, Gavin." He watched as she cradled her new pet in her arms and headed back to her room. The kitten was just a start. After seeing that smile on her face, he knew he'd move mountains to keep it there. Feeling satisfied with the impulsive purchase, he reached for his phone and sent a message to Sheppard.

Gavin:

Headed to the garage. Don't forget to grab the new plugs.

Sheppard:

Damn. Forgot about that. I'll be there when I can.

Gavin:

Everything okay?

Sheppard:

Will be. Gotta see about something, and then I'll head that way.

Gavin:

Here if you need a hand.

While Gavin headed into the garage to get to work, Sheppard was still at home. He'd overheard his wife, Ana, talking on the phone. He could tell by the sound of her voice that something was wrong, and he wouldn't leave until he knew she was okay. It was just the way he was. Sheppard was always looking out for the people he cared about. It was nothing for him to put his life on the line for his family. He'd proven that the day he took a bullet for Bishop. The club was under attack, and when he saw that Bishop was in trouble, he stepped forward, took a shot to the chest, and fell into the river. He would've died if Ana hadn't found him. She saved his life and stole his heart in the process.

He looked over at her, seeing her stare out the

kitchen window as she listened to someone talk on the other end of the line. He stepped closer, trying to see if he could find out what was wrong. After several seconds, she finally said, "I really hate to hear that. I thought he was doing better last night." She paused, then continued, "I'll talk to them as soon as I get there. I'm leaving the house now."

Sheppard could tell by the tremble in Ana's voice that something was wrong, so he waited patiently for the conversation to end. Once she hung up, he asked, "What's wrong, Angel?"

"It's the boy I was telling you about. We got the results back from his brain scan, and it doesn't look good. They've decided to call the family in."

He wrapped his arms around her, pulling her close as he held her. "I hate to hear that, sweetheart. I know you were hoping he'd pull through."

Tears streamed down her face as she told him, "He's so little, Dillon. His parents are going to be heartbroken. It's going to be so hard to tell them."

"I wish there was something I could do." He held her tight, trying to comfort her as she cried. She was one of the strongest women he'd ever known. She'd proven that the day she pulled him out of that river and saved his life. He knew this would be hard for her, but she'd find a way to get through it.

"Being here and loving me is enough. Just keep doing that, okay?"

They'd spent the last year making their new house a home and building a life together. He loved her more than he ever dreamed possible and looked forward to their future together. When the time was right, they'd start their family, but for now, he enjoyed having her all to himself. He kissed her tenderly before he said, "I will always love you, Angel. Nothing will change that."

"I love you, too." She wiped the tears from her eyes and kissed him once more. "I guess I better get going. They're waiting for me."

"I'll be here when you get off. Call me if you need me."

"I will. Have a good one, sweetheart." She kissed him on the cheek and headed for the door.

As soon as she'd gone, Sheppard grabbed his cut and headed for his bike. He had a long day ahead in the garage, and he wanted to be home by the time Ana got off work. After a quick stop in town, he pulled up to the clubhouse. When he got to the garage, most of the brothers were already there. It was their busy season. Christmas was just around the corner, and they had more orders than ever before. The brothers would do whatever it took to get it done, even it meant working overtime. When Sheppard walked into the garage, he took the plugs over to Gavin and then headed over to help Goliath. He was busy working on the hood of one of the old trucks they were restoring.

"You about to get her done?"

"Getting there. Could use a hand."

With a nod, Sheppard set to work. They'd been working for almost an hour when Sheppard looked to him and said, "You never told me what Lily thought of the truck."

"Can't get her out of the damn thing. She loves it. Keeps going on and on about it. Couldn't believe we kept it a secret for so long."

"Good. I'm glad she likes it. Knew she would. Hell, who wouldn't? That truck is badass."

"It is. And it turned out to be a pretty good gift for me, too," Goliath said with a smirk. "She looks hot as hell driving that damn thing."

"I bet she does." He glanced over at the back of the garage and spotted Gavin busting his ass trying to finish an engine breakdown. Sheppard motioned his hand in Gavin's direction. "You think he's ready for tonight?"

"Figure he's feeling a little anxious, but he's gotta know which way we're leaning. He's done what needed to be done to prove himself."

Goliath didn't miss the mischievous look on Sheppard's face as he leaned against the hood of the car and said, "So, he thinks he's got it in the bag, huh?"

"*Shep*. What's going on in that head of yours?"

"Thinking we oughta have a little fun with him, that's all. You know… keep the guy guessing."

"What do you have in mind?"

"Just follow my lead," Sheppard told him as he

headed in Gavin's direction.

Goliath followed close behind and almost felt sorry for Gavin as he heard Shep say, "We know."

Gavin's eyebrows furrowed with confusion as he stood up to face Sheppard. "Know what?"

Sheppard watched with amusement as Goliath stepped over to Gavin and gave him an angry glare. "We fucking *know*. And it's all gonna come out tonight. You can count on that."

Gavin's mind started to race as he tried to figure out what they were talking about. He couldn't think of what he might have done wrong. "I don't know what you're talking about."

"Sure you don't," Sheppard barked. "You think you can pull that shit and none of us would find out? You got another thing coming, Knuckles."

They both turned and walked away, leaving Gavin dazed and confused. He couldn't imagine what he'd done to make them so angry. He ran his hands over his face as his mind raced with a million thoughts. He'd walked a straight line and tried to do whatever was expected of him. He couldn't think of a time when he'd screwed up, even when it came to Sunny. It took all his restraint to keep from kissing her the other night. If she was ever that close to him again, he didn't think he'd have the strength to hold back. He wanted her. There was no denying that, but he couldn't act on his feelings. At least not yet.

A sly smile spread across Goliath's face as he watched Gavin start to pace back and forth. He chuckled under his breath as he picked up his sander. "You know he's going to worry about that shit for the rest of the day."

"That's the point. Gotta keep him guessing." Sheppard chuckled as he looked over at Gavin. "Did Maverick make it in yet?"

"Yeah. They got in late last night. Lily's with them now."

"Good. It's going to mean a lot to Gavin that they're here. Anything I can do to help?"

"I think we've got it. They're planning to head back tomorrow afternoon. Maverick's gotta get back."

"And everything is set for tonight?"

"Yeah. Brandy and the girls have a big blowout planned, not that Gavin's going to go for that. He's got it pretty bad for Sunny, and once he gets that patch, maybe he'll actually do something about it."

Goliath turned on the sander and while he finished prepping the hood, Sheppard started working on the side panels. Bull and Renegade worked together to break down the engine piece by piece, making a list of parts they'd need replaced as they went. Renegade was only gone on his honeymoon for a couple of weeks, but his time away had been costly. His brothers fell behind without him, and Renegade was determined to get them caught back up. With Gavin and Bull's help, he knew it would only be a matter of time before they were back on track.

While they were all working on their next project, their president was in his office with an unwelcome guest.

Bishop leaned back in his chair as he looked over at the sheriff. "So, what brings you out here today, Paul? You finally gonna do something with that old Harley of yours?"

"I've been aiming to bring it out here, but something always seems to come up. I'll get around to it before long."

"So, what can I do for you?"

"Been looking over Sunny's case. After a year, we still haven't had any leads on Drew Cartwright's whereabouts. His parents and the DA are pushing for some answers. They're pressing hard on this, and I've gotta give them something. I need to talk to Sunny, but before I do, I thought I'd check in with you. See if you remembered anything else from that night."

Bishop reached into his pocket for a cigarette, lighting it before he replied, "Already told you everything, Paul. Not much else to say. And she's told you everything she knows. There's no sense in stirring things up with her."

"I figured you'd say that. I'm not trying to upset the girl, but I need some answers. You gotta admit, it's strange that no one has seen him after all this time."

Bishop shrugged his shoulders with no response. "His folks are adamant that they haven't seen him since the night he attacked Sunny—to the point that they are worried that something happened to him. It's like the guy just disappeared."

"Really, I figured that was a good thing." Bishop crossed his arms. "If the guy has any brains whatsoever, he'll never show his face around these parts ever again."

"You said there was no sign of him when you got to the bar that night. Is that right?"

"It is. Sunny was there alone, beat all to hell, so I got her to the hospital. That's all I know. I've got no idea where the motherfucker is."

"I'm not giving up on this. He's gotta pay for what he did to that girl, Bishop."

"Agreed, and you know, if I had any idea where he might be, I would've already told you."

The sheriff stood up and extended a hand. "I won't keep you then. You know how to reach me."

Bishop shook his hand and followed him to the door. "I'll give you a call if anything comes to mind. And you bring that bike in soon. Let us fix her up for ya."

As soon as he was gone, Bishop walked back over to his desk and dropped into his chair. He sighed as he ran his hands through his hair with frustration. He knew that Sunny talking to the sheriff wouldn't be a good idea. A lot of time had passed, and it was almost behind them. He knew if the sheriff talked to Sunny, there would be a chance it might dredge up memories that she'd locked away during the night of the attack. He couldn't let that happen. Her memories needed to remain exactly where they were: forgotten.

Chapter 5

Katelyn was sitting at the foot of Sunny's bed with her makeup sprawled across the comforter and a mirror in her hand. She batted her eyelashes as she applied another layer of mascara. She was still staring at her reflection when she asked Sunny, "What is it with you and Gavin? Do you like him?"

"Maybe, but I'm not so sure he feels the same way. It doesn't really matter. I'm not ready to get involved with someone right now."

Sunny sat across the room at her desk as she watched Katelyn finish getting dolled up. Her friend had gone all out with a sparkly, new top and tight-fitting jeans, and the new highlights in her short blonde hair made her blue eyes seem even brighter than usual. Unlike her best friend, Sunny had chosen to keep it simple and was wearing one of her t-shirts and worn-out jeans with boots.

"First, it's been over a year. It's time for you to move on and let Drew stop screwing with your life. He's done that enough. Take back the control and move on. Find a way to be happy. And furthermore… Gavin totally has the hots for you, and you know it. He can't keep his eyes off of you, and he's always doing all these sweet things for you." She motioned her hand over to the kitten, who was sprawled out on the bed like she owned it, and continued, "And he got you a cat!"

"He didn't get me the cat. He found her and let me have her."

"I doubt it. I bet that poor guy went out and bought that cat just to give it to you. Just look at her. She's too cute and healthy to be some stray kitten. Now, stop worrying so much and get Drew out of your head."

Sunny took a deep breath as she tried to fight the tears that were pooling in her eyes. "It's not that easy. How do I move on when I know he's still out there? What if he decides to come back and finish what he started?"

"He's gone Sunny. He's probably sitting on some beach somewhere drinking. Besides, there's no way he'd come back here. He knows that Bishop and the guys would never let that happen."

"It all makes sense when you say it out loud. It's just all the crazy doubts and fears that keep bouncing around in my head. I just want it to stop. I think I might like Gavin... but I'm afraid I'll just screw it all up."

"You'll never know unless you try, and from what I can tell, it would be pretty damn hard to screw things up with him. He's got it bad for you, girl."

Sunny rolled her eyes and said, "Whatever."

"He does, and you know it." She looked over on the bedside table wanting to put on some tunes. "Where's your phone?"

"I left it on the charger in my car. I'll go get it."

"No, don't do that. I can do without. I'm sure there will be plenty of music at the bar." She tossed her mascara back into her bag and stood up, brushing the lint from her jeans. "I'm all set. Now it's your turn."

"My turn?"

"You heard me. Tonight, you're getting the works, whether you want them or not."

While Katelyn was busy making over Sunny, the brothers were on their way to church. Bishop had called them all together to go over the next month's agenda and other club business. Gavin's nerves were on high alert as he watched his brothers file into the conference room, and seeing Goliath and Crack Nut's angry glares as they passed by didn't help matters. He knew his patch was up for vote, and after his conversation with Goliath and Sheppard, he worried that he might just get shot down. If the club decided to vote against him, he would lose his only chance at becoming a brother. Panic washed over him as he thought that he might have screwed things up, but he would have to wait it out. He knew they had a lot to cover, and his vote would be the last thing on the agenda.

Before Bishop started, he had some important information to share. "The Sheriff came by today."

Goliath looked over at him with concern. "About Sunny?"

"He's not giving up. He has his mind set on finding

Drew. We all know he's got good intentions, but I don't want him stirring up shit, not when she's finally pulling herself together."

"What do you need us to do?" Sheppard asked.

"Be vigilant. Keep your eyes and ears open. If they find anything, I don't want us to be the last to know."

"I'll keep an eye on things," Crack Nut assured him. Hacking into the department's server had never been a problem where he was concerned; he'd always had a way with computers, and even though they hadn't needed his hacking skills in quite some time, they could definitely use him now.

"Let me know if you find something. It's time for Sunny to be able to put this behind her and I don't want anything screwing that up." Bishop took a cleansing breath, trying to push back his concern so that he could move on to the next task at hand. He spent the following hour going over all the new orders that needed to be completed by spring. Seeing how much work they had coming their way, the brothers all agreed it was time to take on a couple of new prospects. They needed the extra help with the garage, and it was what needed to be done if they wanted the club to continue to grow—especially since Gavin was up for vote.

"As you all know, Gavin's patch is up for vote tonight. It's been a year since he started prospecting for us, and I think we can all say that he's shown he would be a good addition to the club. But ultimately, that is up to the vote. So, let's get this thing done. All in favor, say aye." The room immediately filled with an echo of 'ayes' from the brothers of the Devil Chaser's MC. "All that oppose." The room fell silent. Not a single member of the club had qualms with Gavin, and all wanted to call him brother. "Then, it's official. Gavin's in. Now, Goliath and Shep… figure it's time for you two to give the poor kid a break and tell him the good news."

A knowing grin spread across Sheppard's face. "It was all in good fun, Prez."

"I'm sure it was." He shook his head and chuckled as he slammed down the gavel. "Meeting dismissed."

By the time the brothers started to come out of the conference room, Gavin was a complete mess. He'd spent the last hour pacing back and forth as he prayed the vote would go his way. His eyes widened as he watched Goliath start walking in his direction. He studied his expression, trying to decipher his mood.

Gavin clenched his jaw as he listened to Goliath say, "Welcome to the club, brother."

Gavin's eyes widened with anticipation as Goliath handed him his new leather cut. He took it from his hand and held it in the air, admiring the Devil Chaser's logo embroidered on the back. With an overwhelming sense of pride, he pulled it on and said, "Thanks, brother."

Goliath pulled him in for a quick hug and a friendly slap on the back. "Congratulations, Knuckles."

The others followed suit, giving their celebratory hugs and welcomes, and Gavin couldn't have been happier. When Sheppard came up to him, Gavin looked up to him and asked, "So you and Goliath were just fucking with me?"

"Yeah. Needed to keep you on your toes. And it worked. I wish you could've seen your face."

"I was sweatin' it, man. No doubt about that."

"It's all over now." He chuckled as he gave him a quick hug. "You did good. Glad to call you brother."

"Thanks, Shep."

"Now it's time to drink."

They followed the others into the bar. They were all looking forward to a night to let off some steam and celebrate. When Gavin stepped up to the counter, Lily handed him a cold beer and said, "Congrats, Gavin."

"Thanks, Lil." He took a long pull from the beer. He glanced around at all of his brothers and their wives gathered nearby, and his lips curled into a smile as he spotted Maverick and Henley sitting at the end of the bar. He and his brother had been through so much over the past few years, and it meant a great deal to Gavin that they'd been able to put it behind them. Having his brother there made the night seem even more surreal.

As soon as Maverick noticed him walking in his direction, he stood up and started towards him. After everything they'd been through, Maverick never failed to be there for his little brother, and even though it didn't surprise him that he'd come, it still meant a great deal to him. Gavin wrapped his arms around his brother's neck and said, "Thanks for coming."

"Wouldn't miss it, little brother. Proud of you."

He took a step back and looked at his big brother. "It's really good to see you. Both of you."

"Good to see you, too. It's been too long."

They walked over to Henley, and Gavin gave her a tight hug before sitting down next to her. "How's that nephew of mine?"

Henley's eyes lit up at the mention of her newborn son. There was no mistaking her love for him as she said, "He's growing like a weed. I can't believe how big he's gotten over the past couple of months. I can't wait for you to see him."

"Did you bring him along?"

"We did. He's at Lily's with the sitter. You'll have to come by tomorrow before we leave."

Gavin looked over at Maverick. "You're leaving tomorrow? Why so soon?"

"Wanted to stay longer, but couldn't swing it this time."

Henley leaned forward as she said, "Things are a little crazy back at home."

"I know how it is. Maybe the next visit can be longer," Gavin told them hopefully.

They'd been talking for almost an hour when Courtney walked up. Maverick smiled when he saw his old friend and stood up to give her a hug. Just seeing her reminded him of the weeks he'd stayed with her while the Devil Chaser's were under attack. He had been there to protect her, but he ended up developing a soft spot for the spunky redhead. Her smile was contagious, and there was no doubt that she had a way of keeping him on his toes.

"Hey there, guys! I wasn't expecting you two to be here."

"We wanted it to be a surprise. It's good to see ya, Court. Where's Bobby?"

"He's over playing a game of pool with Shep and the guys. Why don't you fellas go join them so us girls can talk for a bit." She sat down next to Henley as she motioned over to Lily for a drink.

"Let's go, bro. Leave the ladies to their idle gossip." Maverick gave Henley a quick kiss on the forehead. "I'll be back in a bit."

As they made their way over to the pool tables, Gavin spotted Sunny. She was sitting at one of the tables with Katelyn, and they were talking to Levi and Conner. Sunny looked over to him and smiled, and everything around him stilled. He'd never seen her look so beautiful. It wasn't the new clothes or the makeup. It wasn't even the different way she'd done her long, auburn hair. It was that spark in her eyes when she smiled at him that made his heart hammer against his chest. He could've spent the entire night just standing there staring at her and would have if he hadn't heard his brother calling his name.

Sunny watched as Gavin walked by their table. Without saying a word, he went over to join the others playing pool. Disappointment crept over her when he didn't stop to say hello. She'd noticed the way he'd just looked at her and wondered if Katelyn had overdone it with her little makeover. She glanced back over to Gavin and her heart sank as she spotted Brandy making her move by slipping her arm around his waist.

Sensing Sunny's sudden change in mood, Katelyn tapped her on the knee and asked, "How you doing over there, hotness?"

She picked up her drink and took a quick sip. "I'm great," she lied. "Thinking I might go grab another drink. You want one?"

"I'll get it," Conner offered.

Her eyes skirted over to the pool tables one last time, seeing once again that Brandy and her friend, Stacey, were pawing over Gavin and Otis. She quickly looked away and stood up from the table. "No, that's okay. I'll get it. Can I get you guys anything?"

Katelyn's eyebrows furrowed as she asked, "Sunny, what's wrong?"

"Nothing, silly. I'm just going to get a drink. I'll be right back." Before Katelyn had a chance to question her further, she turned and walked over to the bar. She'd just asked Doc for another drink, when she heard Tessa call out her name.

"Sunny! Come sit with us for a minute." Tessa motioned her over to the end of the bar where she was sitting with Henley, Courtney, and Taylor. She felt a slight tightness in her chest as she walked over to all the ol' ladies. Each of them were great one-on-one, but as a group they seemed a bit intimidating.

"Hey, y'all."

Tessa patted the seat of one of the empty stools. "Come over and chat with us. I haven't had a chance to talk to you much lately. Tell me how things are going."

"Ummm... okay." All eyes were on her as she sat down next to Tessa. She gave Doc a friendly smile when he placed her fresh drink on the counter in front of her, then she looked back over at Tessa. "Not much to tell. Things are going good. My finals are in a couple of weeks, and then I'll start the spring semester at UTM."

"Have you decided on a major yet?" Courtney asked. "Please don't say teaching."

Sunny couldn't help but smile. Tessa and Courtney taught at the same school, and even though they both complained at times, everyone knew they loved their jobs. It was obvious by all the crazy tales they told about their students. Sunny's all-time favorite story had always been Tessa's account of the day she'd met Bishop. He'd come to her school for a parent-teacher conference after Myles had gotten in a fight in her class. Even though she tried to deny it, she fell for him from the start, not that anyone could blame her. Bishop was not only handsome, but smart and protective, making those around him feel safer just being in his presence.

"I'm not sure yet, but I don't think teaching is for me. Maybe I'll try nursing or social work." Sunny looked over her shoulder, taking one last look at Gavin, and sighed when she saw Stacey was whispering something in his ear.

When she turned back around, Courtney asked, "What's with the look?"

"What look?"

Courtney leaned back, looking over at the boys playing pool, and groaned. "Oh, I see what's wrong... it's the hoochie momma twins."

Tessa rested her hand on Sunny's shoulder and said, "Sweetie, you don't have anything to worry about with those girls, especially when it comes to Gavin."

Courtney's eyes lit up. "Gavin? You've got a thing for Gavin? How did I not know this?"

A dark red blush rushed over Sunny's face. "No... it's not like that."

"Why not? He's a great guy," Courtney pushed. "And he's so pretty."

Tessa gave Courtney a disapproving look as she said, "Gavin is a great guy, and he obviously thinks a lot of you. Brandy is just..."

"A bag full of dicks. Don't worry about her," Courtney interrupted. "I don't even know why she still sticks around. It might be time for her to get the Cindy treatment."

Taylor laughed out and said, "The Cindy treatment might be a little drastic, Court."

"Wait... what are y'all talking about? What's the Cindy treatment?" Sunny asked.

Tessa looked over to her with a big smile. "Let's just say, Courtney got her revenge on one of the fallen girls who just wouldn't get the hint. She kept messing around with Bobby until Courtney set her straight."

"How'd she do that?"

"I left her a little surprise in her bed. One that left a lasting impression. After that, she steered clear of both of us," Courtney explained.

"You can't leave me hanging like this, Court. What did you leave in her bed?" Sunny pushed.

"Just a big ol' mess of wieners and all kinds of other goodies. I'm sure it took her a while to get the smell out of her room, and looking back, I might've gone a little overboard."

Taylor shook her head and said, "No, she was asking for it. Considering everything, I think you were pretty easy on her. I'm not sure what I would've done if she was like that with Renegade."

Taylor was Renegade's ol' lady, and although Sunny didn't know the full story of how Taylor and Renegade came together, she did know that Taylor's brother was a member of the club who was killed several years ago. They all had a hard time coping with his death, especially Renegade. Ace had been a close friend of his from the beginning, and he'd never really gotten over losing him. As Sergeant at Arms of the club, Renegade had always seemed a little more intense and on edge than the other brothers, unless he was around Taylor. When they were together, he seemed more laidback—happy. They were good together, just like all the other couples. Sunny wanted what they had. She wanted someone who would love her unconditionally and help keep the darkness away.

Sunny tried to fight the urge, but couldn't stop herself from taking another look over in Gavin's direction. Her peek turned into a glare when she saw that he was talking to Stacey. She had no idea what he was saying to her, but the provocative look on Stacey's face made her stomach turn with jealousy. Sunny hated what she was feeling. She knew she had no reason to feel that way. She had no claim to Gavin. He hadn't even asked her out, but that didn't stop that gnawing feeling deep inside her chest.

When she couldn't stand it any longer, she stood up and said, "I'm going to get a little air. I'll be right back."

"You want me to go with you?" Tessa offered.

Sunny sat her drink down on the counter and turned for the door. "No. That's okay. Just need a minute to clear my head."

Chapter 6

When Gavin saw Sunny go out the back door, he knew something must've been wrong. She didn't go outside alone, especially late at night. He leaned his pool stick against the table and started towards the door. He hadn't made it far when Stacey purred, "Where you running off to?"

"Outside."

She took a step in his direction. "Want some company?"

"No."

She curled into him as her hand raked across his chest. "Are you sure? I thought we might spend a little time together... *alone*."

Gavin pushed her to the side and repeated, "No."

His mind was set on finding Sunny as he made his way through the crowd. Before he stepped outside, he looked over at Bishop. He knew that getting his patch changed things. He was now part of something bigger than himself—a brother, and no different than the others. But he still wanted his president's approval before he stepped out that door. Bishop had always known how Gavin felt about Sunny and trusted that he would be good for her, but in his own way, he'd let him know that the time just wasn't right. They'd all seen that she was finding her way back, and he hoped it was enough.

Bishop had seen Sunny go out the back door, and he'd also seen why. He looked over at Gavin as he thought about his next move. He thought about all those years living next door to Sunny, seeing her grow into the woman she had become. He'd seen her go on her first date, to her first prom, and get her first car. He was there for the best times in her life, and he was there at her worst. There was no doubt in his mind that Gavin cared for Sunny, and when he saw the concern in Gavin's eyes, he knew in his gut that it was time to hand over the reins. He gave him a slight nod, letting Gavin know he had his consent to go after Sunny.

With that, Gavin stepped out into the cold night air and called out to her. "Sunny?" When he didn't get an answer, he called out her name again, only louder. "Sunny!"

As he started for the back of the building, he heard, "Gavin?" He quickly turned and relief washed over him when he saw that she was okay. A puzzled look crossed her face as she saw him standing there. "What are you doing out here? You should be inside celebrating with the guys."

He walked over to her and said, "I'm exactly where I want to be."

"You want to be outside in the freezing cold?"

"No... I want to be out here with you."

Sunny hadn't expected to hear that from him. Why would he want to be out here with her when Stacey obviously planned to show him a good time? There had to be a reason, so she furrowed her eyebrows and asked, "Why?"

He brought his hands up to her face, resting his palms along her jaw as he tilted her head up towards his. "There's no one I'd rather be with than you. No one."

Her heart started to race as he lowered his head and placed his mouth against hers, kissing her ever so softly. With just one touch of his lips, her entire body turned to putty. All her past fears began to slowly fade. She wanted to feel his touch—to kiss and be kissed. He pulled her closer as he deepened the kiss, sending her on a high like she'd never felt before. She relished the warmth of his body next to hers, and she wanted more. The alluring scent of his cologne and the tingling sensation that rushed through her body made her hungry for his touch. Just as the kiss became heated, Gavin took a step back. All his doubts quickly diminished when he looked down at her and saw the lustful look in her eye. Still, he needed to hear it from her.

"Wanna tell me what you're doing out here all alone?"

Her eyes dropped to the ground while she considered her answer. He had been right. She'd been totally wrong about him. The kiss and everything he'd said proved that, but now she wasn't sure how to respond. Feeling a bit overwhelmed, she answered, "I just needed to get some air, but I'm good now."

He placed his hands on her hips, pulling her closer to him. "It didn't have anything to do with Stacey?"

"Maybe a little."

"Gotta give me more than that, Sunny. Why did Stacey get to you?"

"Because she was throwing herself at you."

"And?" he pushed.

"And... I didn't like it. I know it's crazy... It doesn't make any sense at all. It's not like I had any reason to feel that way. I mean, we weren't even really talking ... but in my mind, I'd kinda claimed you as *mine*, and I didn't like her..."

Her words spurred something deep inside of Gavin, making him lose all sense of restraint. He dropped his mouth to hers, silencing her words with another kiss, but this kiss was different from their first. It was intense and full of need, sending the heat of desire rushing through them both. Gavin's tongue brushed against hers as his hands roamed over her body. With just one kiss, he ignited a fire inside of her that she'd never be able to put out. Sunny's nails raked across his back as she pressed her center against his growing bulge. Fearing that he wouldn't be able to restrain himself much longer, Gavin pulled back, releasing Sunny from their embrace. When he looked down at her and saw her flushed cheeks and full lips, he knew. She was everything he wanted and more.

His eyes were locked on hers, making her body tremble under the heat of his stare as he ran his thumb across her bottom lip. "Fucking incredible."

Being so close to him made her mind spiral out of control. She couldn't stop thinking of all those little moments that she'd misinterpreted. She'd been wrong about so many things, and now that she was in Gavin's arms, she saw what she'd been missing. When he felt her shiver, he asked, "Are you cold? Do we need to go back inside?"

"Not just yet. Can we stay out here for just a minute longer?"

"Yeah, we can do that." He took her hand and led her over to the fire pit. She waited patiently as he threw several logs in and started a fire. Once he was done, he walked back over to her and asked, "How's the kitten?"

"She's good. It's nice having her around." She thought back to what Katelyn had said earlier, and she was curious to see if she was right. "Where did you get her?"

"At the shelter downtown."

"Why didn't you just tell me?"

"I wanted to do it for you. Thought you might like some company when you were studying. I didn't want to complicate things by making a big deal of it."

She reached for his hand, lacing her fingers through his, and stared into the fire. "I can't believe how wrong

I was about everything. I thought you hated me, and that you were just doing all those things because you had to."

"Why would I ever hate you, Sunny?"

"I don't know. Maybe because I almost got myself killed by getting involved with a psychopath and basically screwing up my life."

Shocked by her statement, Gavin turned to face her. "I don't see it that way at all. I think you're amazing. You survived. You fought to get your life back and won. Each day you're getting stronger, and soon, nothing will stop you. Not many people would be able to do that."

"I've been lucky, and I haven't done it all alone. I've needed a lot of help."

"You were lucky… extremely lucky. And you were smart to take the help. We all have a past, Sunny. God knows I have mine. I've made my share of bad choices, and as much as I would like to forget them, I can't. I'm reminded of them every time JW walks through the door."

"I know it has to be hard, but in the end, you did what was right for your son. JW is happy. Everyone can see that."

"He is, and I have to keep reminding myself of that. I hope one day he'll understand."

"I have no doubt that he will. You loved him enough to let him go. That says it all."

He lifted her hand up to his mouth and gently kissed the back of it. "You're really something, Sunny. Beautiful, smart, and someday very soon, you will be *mine*."

Before Sunny had a chance to respond, Katelyn stuck her head out the back door and yelled, "Hey, woman! I've been looking for you!"

Katelyn stepped out of the door with Conner and Levi following right behind her. Sunny could tell by her friend's lopsided smile and staggering step that she was obviously having a good time with her new friends. When she finally made her way over to Sunny, she took hold of her arm and pulled her closer as she whispered, "What's going on with hottie hot?"

"Nothing. What's going on with you and the guys? Looks like you're having a good time."

"I'm having a very good time. I mean... look at them. They are totally fine with all those muscles and pretty eyes. And oh my god, have you seen their asses in those jeans? They are so damn hot. I could do something really wild and stupid with those two. Like the *legendary* kind of wild and stupid."

"Katelyn," Sunny warned. "You're still getting over things with Justin. Don't do something you're going to regret later."

Her friend pointed over to the handsome brothers standing by the fire and said, "How could I regret a night with them? Besides, it's just a fling. One wild and crazy night to forget that asshole. I have no doubt those two can make me forget just about anything."

"And what happens when you fall for one of them? Or worse, both?"

"It's a one-night stand. I'm not falling for anyone, sweet cheeks. I've got this," Katelyn assured her as she walked over to the guys with one of her sexy smirks. Minutes later, Sunny watched as Conner and Levi led Katelyn into the clubhouse. She was tempted to call out to her, but she knew it wouldn't help; Katelyn had already made up her mind, and there was no point in trying to change it.

Sunny looked over at Gavin and said, "She is *so* gonna regret that in the morning."

"Probably." He wrapped his arms around her, feeling her body tremble against his chest. "It's freezing out here. It's time to get you inside, lucky girl."

She smiled when she heard his new nickname for her. While she wasn't sure she'd ever be able to consider herself lucky, she liked the fact that he did. Just knowing he felt that way gave her a sense of hope. When she thought back to everything that had happened to her, she started to think that maybe everything really did happen for a reason, playing out exactly the way they were supposed to. If she hadn't come to the clubhouse after the attack, she wouldn't have been there with him now, so maybe, just maybe, she was luckier than she'd thought.

She stood nestled against his chest for just a few moments longer and then said, "Okay. I'm ready."

He took her hand and she followed him into the bar. Gavin spotted Bishop watching them as they started walking over to the pool tables. Bishop didn't have to say the words; Gavin knew from the look on his face that he was pleased, and that's all he needed to know. Gavin pulled out a chair, and Sunny was just about to sit down when she turned to him and said, "Crap. I forgot my phone in my car. I'll be right back."

"I'll get it."

"No. That's okay. You don't have to do that. I've got it. Besides, your brother will want to see you before they have to leave. I'll be two minutes."

"I'll get it. Just stay put. I'll be right back." He kissed her on her temple, and as he started for the door, Maverick called out his name. He peered over towards the bar and noticed his brother motioning him over. He looked back at Sunny and said, "Don't move."

She watched as he continued over to the bar, and once he started talking to his brother, she looked to the back door. Thinking that they hadn't seen anyone when they'd been outside earlier, she thought she'd be fine to go out and get her phone herself. She was feeling strong, more confident, and knew she needed to be able to do these kinds of things on her own. She'd be back before he'd even know she was gone, so she headed outside.

She glanced around the dark parking lot and felt certain that there was no one there. Unfortunately, she was wrong.

She opened her car door and quickly leaned inside to get her phone. Just as she stuck it in her back pocket, she heard a deep, angry voice say, "I never understood why he was so fascinated by you. I never could figure out why he couldn't just let you go."

Sunny quickly turned and was horrified to see Drew's father standing there hidden in the darkness. In that moment, everything around her fell away. She didn't hear the hum of cars passing by or the music blaring from inside the bar. She couldn't feel the cold nipping at her nose or the hair prickling on her arms. Everything was on hold, like she was frozen in time. Adrenaline rushed through her veins like an ignited fuse. She couldn't move a muscle, not even to scream. She desperately wanted to cry out for help, but the words wouldn't come. Panic had stolen her voice, but she finally managed to ask, "What are you doing here, Mr. Cartwright?"

As he stepped closer, the security light flickered on, and Sunny's terror immediately started to subside. Drew's father had aged ten years since the night his son had gone missing over a year ago. His eyes were tired and defeated, and in her heart, she knew he wasn't there to hurt her. But that didn't keep her heart from racing against her chest when he said, "I need to know. Please just tell me where he is. I can't keep living like this."

"I don't know, Mr. Cartwright. I still don't remember everything that happened that night. All I know for certain is, I haven't seen Drew since the night at Hidden Creek."

"He's a good boy. He just lost his way because you led him on and made him think you cared about him. You broke his heart."

"And he broke my jaw when he slammed his beer bottle into my face and not to mention my wrist. He almost killed me. So, I'm sorry, but I honestly hope he never comes back here."

"He would've never done all those things you said. Never! It's all lies and you know it."

"Mr. Cartwright, you're wrong. Drew did do all those things to me and more. I don't know what it was, but there was something wrong with him. I didn't want to believe it either, but it's true."

His voice trembled like he was on the verge of tears as he said, "Just tell me where he is... I need to know. I'll never have peace until I know if my boy is alive or dead."

"I've told you... I have no idea where he is."

He advanced towards her and placed his hands just below her shoulders, digging his fingers into her arms. "You're lying!"

She placed the palms of her hands on his chest, pushing him back as she shouted, "Don't do this. Just let me go!"

"Not until you tell me where he is! Just tell me! Where is my *son*?"

Oddly enough, Sunny still wasn't afraid. Mr. Cartwright wasn't like Drew. He wasn't a mean, vile man. He wasn't standing before her in a fit of rage. He was just a father in desperate need of finding his son. The look in his eyes reminded her of her mother. She had the same look the night Sunny was admitted into the hospital—a broken, helpless look that wouldn't go away until she knew her child was okay. Sunny wanted to help him, to tell him where Drew had gone, but she didn't have the answers he needed and she feared she never would.

Chapter 7

Once he'd made it over to the bar, Maverick looked over at his brother and said, "We're heading out. We need to get back and check on Thomas."

"I'll come by to see Thomas in the morning before you go." Gavin gave his brother a tight hug as he said, "Thanks for coming. Meant a lot."

"Proud of you, Gavin. You did good." He gave him a pat on the shoulder and said, "We'll see you in the morning."

As they walked out the door, Gavin looked over at the empty table where Sunny had been sitting, and a sick feeling twisted in his gut when he realized she'd gone outside alone. It'd only been a few minutes, but in his heart, he knew something wasn't right. He started through the crowd, ignoring the calls of his brothers as he charged towards the back door.

His mind was too consumed with worry to answer, so he just kept going. When he finally made it to the parking lot, his fears came to life when he heard Sunny yelp, "Let me go!"

When he turned the corner, he found a man with his hands on his girl. He didn't wait to ask questions. Instead, he grabbed the back of the man's jacket and slung him against the car. He reared back his fist and slammed into the man's face, making him fall back onto the hood of Sunny's car. Just as he was about to hit him again, Sunny reached for his arm and pleaded, "Stop."

Gavin froze. She stepped in front of Mr. Cartwright and told him, "You need to go, Mr. Cartwright. We don't know anything about your son."

With his hand pressed against his face, he pulled himself up off the car. It took him a moment to get his footing, but eventually he started staggering back towards the gate. He hadn't gotten very far when Bishop and Goliath appeared. Bishop turned to Gavin and asked, "What happened?"

"Cartwright." Tension rolled off Gavin as he glared at the gate and growled, "How the fuck did he get in here?"

"Fucking prospect let him in," Bishop growled. "Rookie mistake. Cartwright told him he was here to pick up his truck. He said a bunch of bullshit about traffic in Kentucky holding him up, making him late. Our guy told him to wait by the gate until I got there." Concern flooded his face as he walked over to Sunny. "You okay? Did he hurt you?"

"No. I'm fine." Sunny was pleased with herself. Even with being out in the dark with a man who threatened her, she'd managed to keep it together. She could see the doubt in Bishop's eyes, so she said, "Really. I'm okay."

"Get her back inside," Bishop demanded. He

motioned for Goliath and they both started towards the gate. "We need to make this short. He gets nothing from us."

Goliath nodded as they continued to pursue Drew's father out onto the side road. When they turned the corner, they saw that he was about to get into his car. Before he had a chance to leave, Bishop yelled, "Cartwright!"

Cartwright wasn't sure if he should just get in his car and leave, or face them now. Either way, he'd screwed up when he put his hands on Sunny. There was no way they were just going to let it go. He'd heard the stories about the men that belonged to the Devil Chaser's MC and what they were like, and he didn't trust any of them. He knew these men were protecting Sunny, but he'd yet to find out what they were hiding. He turned to face the president of the club and grimaced when he saw his leather jacket and tattoos. Bishop was a bigger man than he'd remembered and couldn't help but feel intimidated by his presence.

"I shouldn't have come here. I know that now."

Bishop continued in his direction, fighting the urge to end him on the spot. "No. You shouldn't have, and you sure as hell should've kept your distance from Sunny."

"You don't know what it's like. He was my only son, and now, he's gone. I don't know what I'm supposed to do here."

"You've gotta pull yourself together. Your son made his own choices and never gave a damn about the consequences. It's all on him."

"What do you mean *it's all on him*?" Cartwright bellowed.

"It's time for you to go home, Paul. Put this thing to rest."

It wasn't that easy for Mr. Cartwright. He was a man desperate to find his son. One way or another, he was determined to find his son and prove his innocence. His heart told him there was no way his son could've hurt Sunny the way she'd said he had. It was all lies, and he was determined to make it right.

Bishop gave him a threatening look, and when he noticed the big brute behind him, he knew he was no match for them. "This isn't over."

Ignoring him, Bishop turned and headed back to the bar with Goliath. He knew there was no sense in arguing with Drew's father. There was nothing he could say that would make him give up on finding his son— which meant that they needed a plan. When they got back to the bar, things were starting to die down. After he let Gavin and Sunny know that he'd handled things with Cartwright, he sat down at the bar next to Tessa and the girls. Without looking in his direction, Tessa leaned into him, nestling into the crook of his arm. From the start, they'd always been in sync. She always knew whenever he was close, and he was the same with her.

He listened as they discussed what each of them were bringing to Thanksgiving Dinner, and when Courtney mentioned that she was going to bring a coconut pie instead of her traditional chess, Bishop spoke up.

"No, you can't bring *that*," Bishop told her, sounding bossier than he'd meant to.

Courtney leaned forward and with a puzzled look asked, "What? You don't like coconut pie?"

"The holidays aren't the time to try new recipes, Court. Your chess pie has always been incredible. Why would you want to mess with that?"

"I don't know. I just wanted to try something different."

"Have you ever made a coconut pie?" he pushed.

"No, but I'm pretty sure that I can make one without gagging anyone."

"Not worth the chance. Bring the chess... and some of those cream cheese do-dobbers you make. And have Bobby make that nacho dip stuff he makes for the ball game. I'll get the chips."

"Okay. I'll bring the chess, the pinwheels, and the dip," she conceded. "But I'm bringing the coconut pie, too."

"I'm good with that," Bishop chuckled as he looked over at Tessa. "You about ready?"

It was getting late. Tessa knew Izzie and Sadie would be sound asleep by now, but Myles and Drake were a different story. She had no doubt they'd still be up playing some video game or texting. They'd just hit those wonderful teenage years, and their world was wrapped up in their phones. Thankfully, Izzie was only ten and Sadie was just a few months away from turning two, so they still had a little while before they'd have to worry about teenage girls in the house.

After taking one last sip of her drink, Tessa stood up and gathered her things. "If you think of anything else we might need, just give me a call."

"Just don't get in a frenzy about making everything perfect like you did last year. If we don't have something, we'll send the boys after it or we'll do without. But either way, it won't be a big deal," Courtney fussed.

"I didn't get in a frenzy!"

Courtney rolled her eyes and then looked over to Bishop. "Did she or did she not have a meltdown over the stupid butter?"

Bishop shrugged. "It wasn't all that bad," he lied. "I don't even remember there being a problem with butter."

"Cole Bishop! You know damn well that your wife had a total come-apart over the freaking butter. She thought Thanksgiving was ruined because we didn't have enough. Which we did, by the way."

Tessa elbowed her friend in the side. "I did not have a come-apart, *Courtney*. I was a little worried, that's all. Now, drop it."

"I'll bring the extra butter," Taylor laughed. "Don't want to take any chances."

Tessa looked at her husband with a feigned pout. "Thanks for having my back there, Prez."

He leaned towards her, placing his mouth close to her ear. The heat of his breath sent chills down her spine as he whispered, "I'm sure I can find a way to make it up to you."

"I'm sure you can," she purred. "Bye, girls."

After Bishop and Tessa were gone, the party quickly dwindled. Lily turned the bar over to Doc so she and Goliath could follow Maverick and Henley back to their house. Soon after, the other couples followed suit. It was just the tides of change within the club. Their families were growing, and while they still enjoyed coming together to have a few drinks, the all-night partying had become almost nonexistent. They enjoyed the parties, but the brothers knew there was a time for play and a time for work.

Unlike some, Gavin's mind wasn't on the work he had to do the following morning or the run he had to make at the first of the week. His mind was set on one thing and one thing only: Sunny.

Sunny's eyes were wide with worry when she said, "I'm sorry. I shouldn't have gone outside like that. I should've listened to you."

"No, you shouldn't have gone outside alone."

"I was just feeling good about things. I thought I

could handle it myself."

"I'm glad you are feeling better. That's all I've wanted, but that's not the point. I told you to stay put. Things could've turned out very differently back there. He could've really hurt you."

Her eyes dropped to the ground. "I know. I screwed up."

Gavin reached for her hand as he said, "It's my job to keep you safe. Not just because of the club, but because I take care of what's mine. I'll do whatever it takes, but I need you to do your part."

She looked up at him. "Okay. I'll listen next time. Promise."

"Good. Now let's get a drink," he told her as he took her hand and led her over to the bar.

They'd been sitting in the bar for almost an hour talking and laughing when Sunny decided it was time to find a song to play. He watched as she stood over the old jukebox and searched for the next perfect song. She bit her bottom lip as she strummed her fingernails along the glass. Eventually, there were a few clicks followed by the low rumble of an old country song. Gavin smiled when he realized it was one of his favorites. With a satisfied smile on her face, Sunny started back towards the table.

Before she reached him, Gavin stood up and headed towards her. "Can't play a song like this and not dance to it."

"You like this one?"

"One of my favorites."

"Hmmm. Lucky pick, I guess."

"Reckon so, lucky girl," he told her as he pulled her close.

He'd never been one for dancing. He could remember goofing around the living room with his mother as a kid, but since then, he'd had no interest in ever doing it again—until tonight. He'd use any excuse to be close to Sunny, even dancing with his two left feet. A low, soft melody filled the room as they curled into each other's arms and started to sway to the rhythm of the music. Sunny rested her head against his chest as he wrapped his arms around her waist. She was intoxicated by the scent of his cologne and the touch of his cheek against hers. She could feel the desire building inside her as one song rolled into the next. The sun was just a few hours from rising when Gavin finally said, "I wish I could do this all night, but it's getting late. I've gotta leave first thing in the morning to head out to Montana, and then over to Oregon for parts. As much as I hate the idea, I better get you back to your room."

"Okay."

He took her hand and led her down the hall. Once they were standing at her door, Sunny became extremely anxious. Gavin's perfectly toned body and striking good looks suddenly made her feel intimidated. When she thought about them making love and being naked in front of the sexy man of steel, her insecurities took over. She started doubting her looks and her abilities, especially since she didn't have much experience with sex. In fact, she'd only been with two men—one being an experiment with Katelyn's older brother when she was a sophomore in high school, which ended up being a very awkward mistake for them both, and then there was Drew. She'd been with him several times, but often referred to him as the two-pump chump. He was quick on the draw, and there were definitely no bells and whistles where he was concerned.

She didn't know Gavin's history with women, but she figured he had more experience than her. He did have a son, and even though she'd never actually seen him with any of the club's girls, she assumed he'd been with them. Her eyes widened with embarrassment when she realized she'd been standing there staring at him without saying a word. She inhaled quickly, trying to gather her nerve, and then said, "You wanna come inside?"

"When I come in that room for the first time, there won't be a single doubt left in your mind. All those fucked-up thoughts you just had running through your head will be gone, and you'll know without a doubt that I want that sexy little body of yours. You'll know just how bad I want to taste you… feel you… have my cock buried deep inside you." The warmth of his breath caressed her neck as he lowered his head close to her ear. "When the time is right, you won't be thinking of anything except how much you want me, and you'll be begging for it. Then and only then, I'll come into this room. For now, I'll wait." He dropped his lips to her, kissing her softly. "I'll wait as long as it takes."

Sunny watched as Gavin turned and started down the hall towards his room. "Goodnight, Gavin."

"Night, lucky girl."

She kicked off her boots as she closed the door behind her, then crawled into bed. Without taking off her clothes, she laid her head down on the pillow and pulled the comforter over her legs. She curled to her side, closed her eyes, and spent the next hour replaying everything that had happened that night with Gavin. For the first time in months, Sunny fell asleep with a smile on her face and the nightmares didn't come.

She was still in a deep sleep when Katelyn snuggled up in the bed next to her. When she rolled over, Katelyn raised her eyebrow and said, "Don't ask."

"How can I not ask, Kat? Seriously. You've gotta tell me something here. Are you okay? Did you have fun? Did you fall for one of them?"

She rolled her eyes and laughed as she answered, "I'm fine. I'm a tad overstimulated, but fine."

"So, you did it. You actually went through with it?"

"Yeah, I guess I did. Probably wasn't the smartest thing I've ever done, but damn… hmm."

Feeling curious, Sunny asked, "Would you do it again?"

"With them? I doubt it. Besides, both of them disappeared on me. I woke up this morning in an empty bed. Not exactly good for the old self-esteem, but it wasn't about that anyway. It was just one night with a couple of hot guys… nothing more than that. It's best to just leave it in the past and forget it ever happened."

"I'm beyond curious, but I think you're right. It's best for everyone to just forget it ever happened, especially when it comes to me. There are some things a friend just doesn't need to know." Sunny laughed. "Get some rest."

Katelyn was quiet for several minutes, and Sunny thought she'd fallen asleep. Just as she closed her eyes, she heard Katelyn whisper, "I think I liked them more than I was supposed to."

Sunny looked at her friend, seeing the heartbreak in her eyes, and asked, "What do you mean?"

"It's hard to explain. It wasn't just about the sex. Really. It was something else. I felt this odd pull to them. It was different for each of them. Conner was so attentive and sweet. Every move he made was about me, making sure that I was taken care of, while Levi was strong and demanding. He pushed me to my limits and left me wanting more. It was the things he'd whisper in my ear… like every fantasy I'd ever had was right there in my reach. I'd never felt anything like that before."

"And what about them? Do you think they've done this sort of thing before?"

"I don't know. I don't think so, but they seemed to be into it. But if either of them wanted to make more out of it, they wouldn't have left me alone in the bed. End of story."

"I'm sure they didn't mean to hurt your feelings. I'm sure they thought it would make it easier. You know how guys are."

"Well, it didn't make me feel better. It made me feel like an idiot for thinking there was some kind of connection between us." She let out a frustrated sigh, then continued, "It doesn't matter. I'm being silly, and I know it. I think it's from the lack of sleep. It's messing with my head."

"It's going to be okay, sweetie. Just forget about it and get some rest."

"It could never work, right? I mean, you read about stuff like that in those smutty romance books, but it never works, does it?"

"Only the three of you can answer that."

Chapter 8

Spending the holidays at Bishop's had become a longtime tradition for Sunny and her mother. When her father died ten years earlier, Bishop opened his doors and welcomed them into his home and into his family. If it hadn't been for him, times like these would've been very different for Sunny and her family, but as always, Bishop was always there for the people he cared about. Over the years, he'd become like a second father to Sunny and Tyler, and Glenda would always feel indebted to him for keeping her family safe. They all loved him and looked forward to spending the holidays with his family, but this year was even more special for Sunny. While they'd talked and texted, she hadn't seen Gavin since the night of the party. He and Otis had been gone on a run to Montana for some special parts the garage needed, and it had taken him longer to get back than he'd anticipated. Sunny found herself missing him even more than she'd expected.

She knew she'd see him later that night, so after she'd spent the morning helping her mother prepare the food, she called Katelyn to come over and help her get ready. They were sitting in her room sorting through all the different outfits she'd brought to wear.

"What is going on with you? You've never been

one to worry about what you're wearing."

Sunny stood in front of her full-length mirror and grimaced when she saw her reflection. She pulled off her sweater and tossed it on the bed. "I just want to look nice, that's all."

"What was wrong with that? It looked great on you."

"It looked stupid," she answered as she searched her closet for another option.

"Okay... stop." Katelyn stood up and walked over to Sunny, placing her hands on her shoulders as she looked her friend in the eye. "What is going on?"

"I'm just a little nervous."

"There's nothing to be nervous about. You could wear a brown paper sack and he'd think you looked amazing. Now stop acting like a complete psycho and pick something already. I'm starving. By the time we get there, they will have eaten all the good snacks."

"Okay, fine." She slipped on her black hoodie. After one last glimpse in the mirror, she said, "I'm ready."

"Finally."

When the girls made it over to Bishop's house at last, the driveway was full of cars and motorcycles. Other than the addition of a few guys with leather jackets and tattoos, being there was no different than being in any home in the south on Thanksgiving afternoon. The kids were playing outside, fishing at the pond or playing basketball, while the women were huddled around in the kitchen talking and getting things ready for dinner. When the girls walked in, the entire house smelled like cooked turkey and homemade sweet rolls. As soon as they took off their jackets, Sunny and Katelyn jumped in to help get everything prepared. As she set the table with Ana, she tried to ignore her urge to go find Gavin. All the women seemed perfectly content doing their own thing and paid no mind to their men in the living room. Like the others, Sunny was well aware of what the guys were doing. Without looking, Sunny knew Bishop had finished frying the turkey and was sprawled out in his big leather recliner with his daughter Sadie sitting in his lap. Goliath, Sheppard, and Bobby were all gathered around him watching SportsCenter. They were talking and munching on Bobby's famous nacho cheese dip while the other brothers were probably outside building a bonfire for the kids.

Once they'd gotten everything ready, Tessa turned to Sunny and asked, "Do you mind getting the kids for me?"

"Sure, no problem."

Sunny was just about to walk out the door when Tessa shouted, "Tell the guys out back too, please. They are working on tonight's bonfire."

"Okay."

After she'd gotten the kids inside, Sunny headed around back to get Gavin and the others. Otis and Levi were throwing wood into the fire pit while Gavin and Conner restocked the wood pile behind them. Sunny was filled with a mix of nerves and excitement as she walked over to the guys. She was all set to tell the guys to come inside when Gavin noticed her approaching. He stopped what he was doing and watched as she continued towards them.

"Hey, guys. Tessa said dinner's ready."

"Cool," Levi shouted.

Within seconds, the guys had rushed inside, leaving Gavin outside alone with Sunny.

Sunny stared at him with wonder. It just didn't seem possible that she could be as happy as she was at that moment. It seemed so easy for others. She'd seen her friends smiling and laughing with ease or talking excitedly about a new movie they'd seen or a new boyfriend. It just came naturally to them, but since the attack, it hadn't been that way for Sunny. She wanted to be like them, to live without worry and fear, but she couldn't find the peace within her heart. Drew had stolen that joy from her, and she had yet to find it again—until now. She was finding her way back. She'd taken the hard times that were thrown at her and faced them head on. Each day she was getting stronger, and there was nothing that could stand in her way. She was finally starting to see herself through Gavin's eyes, and she liked what she saw.

After several seconds, she finally smiled and said,

"Hey."

His tone was soft and inviting. "Come here, Lucky."

She took a step towards him with no worry of her past, and once he'd wrapped his arms around her waist, there was no worry of her future. With him, she found peace, and that was all that mattered. All her nerves and apprehension melted away as he held her tightly against his chest. She was falling for him, and it felt good—really good.

"About time you got back," she teased.

"If it were up to me, I would've been back days ago."

She looked up at him and smiled. "If we don't hurry up and get inside, Levi and Conner are going to eat all the turkey."

"You think?"

"Did you see how much they ate last year? I don't know where they put it all."

"Okay, we'll go inside, but first..." Every fiber of her being vibrated with anticipation as he slowly lowered his lips to hers. He held her close as he savored the minty taste of her breath and the warmth of her mouth. A soft, low moan escaped her lips as he lowered his hands to her ass, letting them roam freely as he deepened the kiss. There was no denying their connection. From the moment they touched, an electric charge encircled them, forcing them closer. Just as

Sunny's fingers tangled into Gavin's hair, Katelyn stuck her head out of the back door and shouted.

"Move it or lose it, grandma! Your mom is waiting for you!"

Sunny's face flushed red with embarrassment as she quickly pulled from Gavin's embrace. She took Gavin's hand and started pulling him towards the house as she shouted, "We'll be right there!"

"Just so you know, I wasn't done with those lips of yours," Gavin teased.

"Hmph," Sunny muttered as she continued to tug him along. "Well, just so you know, mom saved you a seat with us."

"That's fine. Your mom is cool."

"She knows," she told him as they started up the stairs.

"About us?"

"Yep. So consider yourself forewarned."

"Ahh, it won't be that bad," he tried to assure her.

Sunny stopped when they got to the top of the front porch steps and then turned to face him. "Mom is cool, but she's always been protective. After everything that happened with Drew, things have been hard on her. She worries about everything."

"Can't say I blame her there, but she's got nothing to worry about where I'm concerned."

"I know that, but it's going to take some time for her to warm up to the idea. I haven't even thought about dating anyone, and now I've got the hots for one of Bishop's brothers. To say she's worried is an understatement, but she'll come around. Don't worry."

Sunny placed her hand on the doorknob, and just as she was about to turn it, Gavin said, "So, you've got the hots for me?"

Without turning to face him, she sighed dramatically and answered, "Don't go getting all cocky about it. Now let's go eat."

Before he could tease her further, she opened the door and started walking towards her mother. She and Gavin had barely had time to sit down when Doc stood up to say the blessing. As soon as he was done, the large platters of food were slowly passed from one person to the next until everyone's plate was piled high. The room fell quiet as everyone started to eat, but the silence didn't last for long. Soon, the low rumble of voices grew louder and louder as everyone finished eating and finally had a chance to talk. It was Sunny's favorite part of the meal. She loved listening to the guys' stories about being out on the road and all the places they'd seen, especially Sheppard's tall tales. He never failed to have the entire room laughing. Once all the stories started rolling in and the laughter ensued, Sunny looked over at her mother and smiled. It was good to see her mother happy. It had been a long time since she'd seen a smile on her face, and she prayed that it would stay there.

When her mother noticed her staring, she asked, "Is everything okay?"

"Yep. Everything is good… really, really good."

Glenda leaned forward and looked at Gavin. "It was awfully sweet of you to get that precious kitten for Sunny. She has gone on and on about her."

"Glad she likes her."

"She loves her!" She smiled, then looked over at his empty plate and asked, "Did you get enough to eat?"

He patted his flat, muscular abdomen. "Oh yes, ma'am. I'm as full as a tick. Couldn't eat another bite if I tried."

"I was hoping you would've saved room for some of my Cherry Delight. I remembered how much you liked it last year, so I made a batch special for you."

He quickly twisted in his chair and turned to study the dessert table. "I can always make room for Cherry Delight."

"I'll go fix you some," she offered.

"No, ma'am. I'll get it. What about you two? Do you want some?"

"I'm too full right now. I'll get some later," Sunny answered.

"I'll get mine later, too."

"Suit yourself." He smiled as he stood and headed over to the dessert table. After he served himself a helping, he walked back over to the table and sat down. When she noticed the large serving on his plate, Sunny gave him a mocking look and asked, "Really?"

"What?"

"I thought you were full."

"And? Have you tried your mother's Cherry Delight?"

"Yeah."

"Okay then. Enough said." With a big smile on his face, he took a large spoonful and shoved it in his mouth. "Hmmm. Better than I remembered." Sunny shook her head and laughed as she watched him gobble up the dessert. Her mother gleamed with pride when she noticed his empty plate. "Thanks, Ms. Glenda. It was incredible."

"You are more than welcome, sweet boy. I'm so glad you liked it."

When Tessa and Courtney started taking some of the dishes off the table, the guys got up and headed into the living room. After Sunny and Gavin put their things away, they started for the back door. Before they stepped outside, Glenda called out, "Gavin? Can I talk to you for just a minute?"

Sunny's eyebrows furrowed as she fussed, "*Mom.*"

"It'll just take a minute," she assured him.

"Sure thing, Ms. Glenda." He looked over to Sunny and said, "I'll meet you out by the pond. The boys are out there fishing."

Sunny knew better than to argue. Her mother had something that she needed to say to Gavin, and whether she liked it or not, she was going to say it. "Okay. I'll be out at the dock."

Once she started down the steps, Glenda led Gavin over to the corner of the porch. She leaned against the back rail and said, "I wasn't sure I'd ever see that look on my daughter's face."

"She seems happy."

"She is, and a lot of that has to do with you. I know how you've been looking out for her, and it means a lot to us both."

"There's nothing I wouldn't do for her," Gavin assured her.

"I was hoping you'd say that." Glenda smiled. "You know that she starts school at UTM in the spring."

"Yes, ma'am."

"You also know things haven't been easy for her, but she's getting her life together. She's found her path, and I don't want anything to get her off track."

"What are you trying to say here? Do you want me to stop seeing your daughter?"

"No. Not at all. I'm saying that if you care about Sunny like you say you do, then you will help her follow her dream. Push her when she gets discouraged, be there when she needs someone to listen, and don't make her feel like she has to choose between you and her career."

"I'd never make her choose. I want a future with her, and you can trust that I will always do whatever it takes to make sure she has whatever she needs. *Always*."

"You know, some people have it easy. They graduate high school and go off to college. They meet someone, they fall in love, have a family, and never have a single bump in the road. For others, it's not that easy. They have to work for it. They have to get past all the obstacles that stand in their way. They have to fight to stay on the right path, because it's a long road home. But once they get there, they know how good they've got it, and it's so much sweeter."

"I don't mind taking the long road home as long as Sunny is there in the end."

"Good. Now, you better get over to the dock before Sunny comes hunting us down," she scoffed.

Gavin leaned towards her to give her a quick hug. "I'll never hold her back. You have my word on that."

"Thank you. That's all I'm asking."

It was already getting dark when Gavin started down the steps towards the dock. He hadn't gotten very far when he heard Sunny and the kids playing basketball at the front of the house. He followed the sound of Sunny's laughter over to the basketball net, and he arrived in just enough time to see her zigzag past Tyler and Myles to make her shot. When the ball dropped through the net, she threw her hands in the air and started to dance around as she taunted, "And that's how it's done, boys!"

"Stop braggin', Sunny," Tyler pouted. "We were kicking your butt a minute ago."

"That was a minute ago," Sunny sassed. "Right now, I'm kicking yours!"

Myles walked over to Tyler and put his hand on his shoulder. "Come on, Tyler. We can still get her."

"Need another player?" Gavin offered.

Sunny's lips curled into a wide smile as she said, "Absolutely."

She'd barely gotten the word out of her mouth when Tyler and Myles started to gripe, "No! That's not fair!"

Gavin looked at Myles and asked, "So two against one is fair?"

"Then let's divide up. You and me against Sunny and Tyler."

Sunny bumped her hip against Tyler's as she said, "Come on, little brother. Let's show them how it's done."

"I'm in! We'll cream you guys!" Tyler boasted.

Sunny twirled the ball in her hand and looked over to Gavin with a playful smile. "You sure about this?"

"Bring it on, lucky girl."

Without any further hesitation, she dribbled several times and then charged for the net. The ball flew through the air and swooshed through the basket. Her hands shot up in the air as she shouted, "Two points!"

Myles grabbed the ball. As he started to advance,

Tyler slipped in front of him, stealing the ball from his hands. Like his sister, he stormed forward and tossed the ball towards the net. When he scored, he ran over and gave his sister a high-five. "We got this, sis."

"Oh yeah, we do."

She laughed as she scurried over to Gavin, waving her hands high in the air as she tried to block his shot. His nose crinkled as he lifted his arms above her and aimed for the net. The ball bounced off the rim which gave Tyler his chance to snatch the ball back. Tyler quickly scored again, giving them a lead that continued throughout the game. When it was over and Tyler and Sunny had won, Myles looked over at Gavin and pouted. "Dude, seriously?"

Gavin shrugged his shoulders and raised his hands in defense as he smiled. "What can I say? It's been a while, man."

"You're, like, six-two. How'd you let us lose to a girl?" Myles groaned.

"We'll get 'em next time," Gavin assured him.

Sunny walked over to Myles and wrapped her arm around his shoulder. "You played a good game, bud. You've really gotten better over the past few months."

"I started the last two games," he bragged. "Coach says I have real potential."

"I totally agree." She smiled and gave him a tight squeeze. "I'll bring Gavin to your next game. Maybe he can pick up some pointers."

"I've got one Monday night."

Gavin smiled as he said, "We'll be there."

"Awesome." His attention was suddenly drawn to a rumble of laughter coming from the backyard. He turned to the others and said, "Let's go check out the fire."

They followed Myles around the house and over to the large bonfire where everyone had gathered with their families. They were all nestled in their lawn chairs with thick blankets thrown over their legs. When Tessa noticed the boys walking in their direction, she smiled and motioned over to their chairs she'd put out for them. Once they were settled in their spots, each of them grabbed an old coat hanger and placed a marshmallow on the end before putting it over the flame. Making s'mores was one of Bishop's favorite traditions, and he always made sure there was plenty to go around. Sunny and Gavin joined their friends and spent the next few hours talking and laughing with no worries about the past or the future. They were living in the moment, enjoying their time with their loved ones, and neither of them had any idea that the tides of change were rolling in.

Chapter 9

It was after eleven when Katelyn pulled through the gate at the clubhouse. As soon as she stopped the car, Gavin parked his bike and walked over to them. He opened the door for Sunny and asked Katelyn, "You coming in?"

Her eyes quickly darted over to Levi and Conner when she spotted them walking into the bar. Just like they'd done all night, both Conner and Levi looked over at Katelyn with yearning. It was obvious they all had something on their minds, but no words were ever spoken. Knowing how Katelyn felt, she wasn't surprised when she started shaking her head. "No. I think I better just head home."

"You sure?" Sunny asked.

"Positive. Besides, it's Black Friday! I have some online shopping to do."

Sunny stepped out of the car and stood beside Gavin. "Okay, have fun. You know where I'll be if you need anything."

Katelyn leaned forward and laughed as she whispered, "So… your room or his?"

Sunny rolled her eyes as she shut the car door and followed Gavin to the back. Once they were inside, Gavin asked, "You want to go to the bar for a drink or something?"

"I would, but I've got to get up early to meet Mom."

"Then I'll take a raincheck." He kissed her lightly on her temple and led her down the hallway to her room. Before she opened the door, he pulled her close and kissed her, slow and long. Even though it was brief, when Gavin's mouth touched hers, Sunny felt a jolt down to her bones. When he released her, Sunny's mind started reeling, and she was tempted to ask him to stay. Before she could form the words, he pressed his lips to her forehead and then said, "Good night, lucky girl. I'll see you in your dreams."

Once he was gone, Sunny stepped inside her room and shut the door. She undressed and headed to the bathroom. After turning on the hot water, she stepped inside the shower. As the warm water cascaded down, her mind was filled with thoughts of Gavin and the day they'd spent together. She'd had a really good day with him and enjoyed getting to know him even better. She'd always known he was a good guy. She'd seen how he was with his brothers and JW, but after listening to his stories about his family and his past, she realized there was even more to him than she'd thought. He carried his own scars, deep and hidden, but they were a part of him and made him who he was. She'd always liked him, but now there was something more. That tingling feeling she'd always felt when he was around had changed to a deep longing, longing to see him and be with him. The quick glimpses had become soulful stares that touched her in ways she couldn't even begin to explain. She was falling in love with him—and she was finally starting to see that he loved her, flaws and all.

She turned off the water and got out of the shower. After quickly drying off, she got dressed and headed down the hall towards Gavin's room. With a sense of determination, she knocked on his door and her chest tightened with nervousness as she waited for him to answer. She tried to be patient, but when he didn't answer after several seconds, she pounded on the door again. Seconds later, the door flung open and Gavin stood behind it dripping wet with a towel wrapped around his waist. "Sunny?"

Sunny's eyes dropped to his chest and quickly roamed over his six pack. Her breath quickened when she noticed the defined V hidden beneath the towel. She was completely focused on the wonder of his physique and didn't realize that he was waiting for her to tell him why she was there.

Seeing her standing there with her wet hair and just a t-shirt made Gavin worry that something might be wrong. With concern in his voice, Gavin prompted her again. "Sunny?"

Her eyes shot up to his, and her brain froze. So many thoughts bombarded her mind and she couldn't think of what she wanted to say.

Gavin finally stepped towards her and placed his hands on her shoulder. "Is everything okay? Did something happen?"

Before he could finish his question, Sunny cut him off. She eased up on her tiptoes and pressed her mouth against his, silencing him with the heat of her kiss. She wound her arms around his neck, pulling him closer as his hands curled around her. When he heard the guys coming down the hall, he gently lifted her off the ground and carried her into his room, kicking the door closed behind them. As he lowered her feet to the floor, his mouth dropped to her shoulder. He trailed kisses along the curve of her neck to her ear as he whispered, "Sunny... you're gonna have to say the words, baby."

Without hesitation, she looked up at him and declared, "I want this, Gavin. I want you. I've never wanted anything more."

His towel dropped to the floor and he stood before her in all his glory. She was motionless and in complete awe. She'd never dreamed that a man could look so perfect, but there he was and he was all hers. Her mind was suddenly filled with wonderful, wicked thoughts. There were no doubts or insecurities about her body or experience. Her mind was completely on him as his mouth covered hers with a kiss that was hungry and demanding. A moan of pleasure filled the small room as his hands drifted to her ass, pulling her tightly against his muscular frame. She felt herself being led backwards as his strong hands slid up her back, pulling the soft cotton t-shirt over her head. When the back of her legs touched the edge of the bed, he slowly lowered her down onto the mattress and tossed her shirt to the side. Her breath became ragged with anticipation as her body begged impatiently for his next touch.

He looked down at her, watching hungrily as her breasts rose and fell with each heaving breath. She gasped as his fingertips gripped her thighs and parted her legs to sink between them. His soft lips hungrily dropped to her breast, raking his tongue across her sensitive nipple. Her ragged breaths echoed through the room as his hand slowly slid between her legs. He ran his thumb along the edge of her lace panties, teasing her and touching her where she wanted him the most. He took his time caressing her while his free hand cupped her breast. The rough, calloused pad of his finger stroked her as he growled, "So fucking perfect."

His mouth moved back to her perfectly round breast, swirling her nipple with his tongue before taking it in his mouth and sucking hard. He alternated between her breasts over and over, all while lowering her black lace panties down her long, lean thighs. He gently tugged them with agonizingly slow movements, reveling in the impatience building within her. Her hands raked through his hair as she pulled his mouth closer.

The storm of delicious sensations flooding through her was almost too much to bear. She could feel the smooth fabric of the lace slipping over her skin as her panties finally reached her ankles. The warmth of his breath caressed her skin as he began to shower her abdomen and thighs with kisses. Her body began to tingle in anticipation as the bristles of his beard brushed against her center.

"Gavin," she whimpered as her hands dropped to the sheets, clamping down. She felt his tongue sweep against her and his fingers ease inside her as his tongue swirled around her most sensitive spot. Her head flew back in pleasure while he continued to tease her with his mouth. She was close to the edge when her hands drifted to his head, her fingers tangling in his hair as she panted, "Yes," over and over again.

She was close, very close to finding her release. She knew a small moment of panic when Gavin lifted up and took a condom from his side table. She fought it back down though. This was Gavin. She was more than safe with him. She waited impatiently as he rolled it down his long, thick shaft, and she'd barely had time to catch her breath when he was back on top of her, centering himself between her legs. She smiled with satisfaction as the tip of his cock brushed against her clit, sending lust-filled chills down her spine. Their naked bodies pressed against each other, his hot skin against hers.

Their eyes met and everything stilled. For so long, her life had been filled with chaos and uncertainty, but in his arms, she felt anchored and secure. There was no denying their connection; Gavin had always known it would be this way. He'd watched her from afar for so long, and now she was in his arms, in his bed, and he was about to claim her in the most absolute way. When he looked at her, there was no doubt in his mind that he loved her more than he ever dreamed possible, and he had every intention of loving her like no one else could.

His lips pressed against hers as his warm hands roamed all over her naked body, leaving a trail of sparks in their wake. She opened her legs wider as he slowly slid inside her, making her breath catch in her throat. Seeing that she needed time to adjust, he stilled and kissed her along the curve of her neck and shoulder. Seconds later, he felt her nails bite into his hip as she rocked her hips against him, urging him to move. He pulled back and entered her again, slow and steady. Instinctively, she arched into him as he drove deeper and gasped as his cock rubbed against her G-spot. She couldn't keep her nails from clawing into his back. Her body had never felt such unrelenting pleasure. He was everything she'd dreamed about and so much more. His mouth once again found hers as he thrust forward again and again, claiming what was his. Waves of ecstasy crashed over her until the dam finally broke and her body was flooded with the all-consuming rush of her climax. He continued to drive into her, deeper and deeper, until he found his own release. With one last thrust, a satisfied growl permeated through the room.

His breaths were ragged and deep as he dropped his head to her chest. With Sunny beneath him, flushed and sated, he'd never felt so content. She was everything he'd ever imagined and so much more. He'd found the love he'd been looking for. He'd found his home with her. With his hands drifting along the side of her hips up to her waist, he whispered, "Mine."

Her nails lightly trailed the length of his back as she responded, "Yes. I'm yours."

He slowly rolled to his side and got out of the bed. Sunny couldn't help but admire his ass as he walked to the bathroom to dispose of the condom. When he got back into bed, he pulled her gently over to him as his head fell against the pillow. She immediately curled into his side and rested her head on his shoulder. His fingers softly brushed through her hair as he said, "Enjoyed tonight."

"I did too," she confessed.

"Didn't realize you were such a good ball player."

"I'm alright, I guess. I've had a lot of practice playing against the boys."

"You know I'm gonna have to have a rematch at some point."

"You sure about that?" she asked. "We beat you pretty bad tonight."

"Absolutely. I just needed a little time to shake off the cobwebs. Next time, I'll be ready."

"I'm sure you will be. I'll try to take it easy on you, just in case," she teased.

"You know you're asking for it, right?"

"Any time. Any place. You name it."

"Alright then. Sunday afternoon, and this time I get Tyler on my team."

"Deal."

"And if we win, you gotta get your mom to make some more of that dessert stuff she brought today."

"You're not going to win, but I'll get her to make you some anyway. And she sent the leftovers home with Levi and Conner."

"Damn."

"She told them it was green bean casserole so they wouldn't eat it."

He lifted himself off the bed and reached for his jeans. "That doesn't mean shit. Those two will eat anything."

Sunny laughed as she watched him quickly buckle his pants. "What are you doing?"

"Come on," he urged. "We've gotta beat them to it."

"You're kidding me. Right now? After what we just did?"

"Yes! Especially now. A man needs to build his stamina." He leaned over and kissed her on the lips. "I'm not done with you just yet."

"Huh?"

"Baby, I'm just getting started."

Chapter  10

Two Weeks Later.

The parking lot was completely full as Sunny drove down each aisle looking for an empty parking space. With a quick look in her rearview mirror, she could see that Bull was trailing close behind on his bike. Knowing that he must be getting frustrated with her, she let out a deep sigh as she looked over to Katelyn and said, "This is insane. I don't think I've ever seen it like this."

"It's not that bad." She sat up in her seat and pointed to an empty space in the last row. "Hey! There's a good one."

"A good one? It's a mile from the door."

"Stop pouting and just get the spot before someone else grabs it." Once Sunny parked the car, Katelyn opened her car door and said, "We'll get what you need and then we'll be done."

"It's not that easy." Sunny grabbed her purse and locked the doors to the car. "I have no idea what I'm getting him. He's given me no hints whatsoever, and I'm going to end up buying something he hates, and I'll never hear the end of it."

"Why didn't you just ask him what he wants?"

Sunny's eyebrows furrowed as she stared down her friend. "Because that takes the fun out of it."

"And searching high and low for the ever-so-perfect gift is fun?"

"No, but at least he'll be surprised when he gets it." Sunny pulled out her phone and started a text message. "I'll ask Mom. Maybe she'll have some ideas."

While Sunny waited for her mother's response, Katelyn told her, "He's a teenager. Give him some money or a gift card and forget about it."

"I want to get him something he will really like." When her mother didn't have any suggestions, they started walking towards the front door. Sunny glanced behind her, and like always, Bull was there walking just a few yards behind her. She giggled under her breath when she noticed several women staring at him as he walked by. She couldn't blame them; he looked good in his cut, a worn-out pair of jeans, and big black boots. His dark brown hair had grown longer, almost resting on his shoulders, and his beard was thick. When he noticed her looking in his direction, he gave her a quick chin-lift and a smile.

After smiling back, she turned to Katelyn and said, "I guess we'll just have to look around. I'll know it when I see it."

"What about Gavin? Have you gotten him something?"

Her lips curled into a smile as she answered, "I got his ordered last week. It should be here on Friday."

"Well? What did you get him?"

"It's a surprise. You'll have to wait and see."

"What? Are you serious? I'm your best friend. We don't keep secrets."

"Sorry, but it ain't happening. I can't take any chances on you running your mouth."

"You suck, you know that, right?" Katelyn huffed.

"Yep. But you'll love me when you see what I got *you* for Christmas."

Curiosity immediately washed over Katelyn. "Oh yeah? What did ya get?"

Without looking in her friend's direction, Sunny replied, "Like I'd ever tell you. You're just going to have to wait, chick, but I promise it will be worth it."

"I guess I can wait," Katelyn giggled. "I almost forgot to tell you… guess who called me last night?"

"Who?"

"Justin. I haven't heard a word from him in weeks, and then he calls and tries to act like nothing's wrong."

"What a jerk."

"He wanted to see me. Said he had some things he needed to say."

"And? What did you tell him?"

"I told him he could forget it. I'm not meeting up with his sorry ass. Besides, he's probably got the clap after being with that ho-bag, Kim. I don't want to be around that."

"The clap? Seriously?" Sunny snickered.

"Or worse! There's no telling what he's got."

"Maybe he just wants to say he's sorry."

"He is sorry. He's a sorry piece of shit, and I don't want anything to do with him. End of story," Katelyn snapped. "What about a new basketball?" she suggested, starting towards the sports section of the store.

They spent the next hour searching for Tyler's Christmas present. Sunny was about to give up and take Katelyn's advice about the gift card when she came across a pair of headphones she knew her brother had been pining over for months. As soon as she saw they were on sale, she boasted, "Heck yeah. He's going to love these!" She turned behind her and held up the headphones as she shouted, "Hey, Bull? What about these?"

But Bull didn't answer. His focus was on a woman who was standing just a few feet away from Sunny. She was thin with long blonde hair and had a baby in her arms. He'd never seen the girl before, but she caught his eye when he noticed that she'd been following Sunny and Katelyn since they'd walked into the store. Aisle after aisle, the girl had been there. At first, he blew it off, thinking that it was just a coincidence, but something about the way she was staring so intently at Sunny got under his skin. He took a step towards her and was just about to ask what she was doing when he heard Sunny shout, "Hey, Bull! Do you think he'll like these or not?"

He turned to look at her, seeing the box of headphones in her hand and answered, "Yeah. Those would be good. I think he'll really like 'em."

When Bull turned back, the girl was gone. Oblivious to Bull's concern, Sunny smiled as she shouted, "Awesome. I think these will work."

"Finally! Grab those babies up and let's get out of here before I lose my mind."

"Don't be so dramatic. It hasn't been that bad," Sunny scolded. "Even Bull found himself a few things."

"Are you kidding me?" She took a step closer. "Did you see those two women fighting over sheets? I mean, I could understand it if we were talking about a great deal on a cell phone or a computer, but sheets? That, I just don't get."

"People need sheets, too."

"Pfft. They don't need them that bad," she sassed as they made their way up to the checkout lane. Once they were done, they all headed out to the parking lot. "So what are you and Gavin up to tonight?"

"I think we're going to the movies. I've been wanting to see that new *Ouija* movie or the new JK Rowling movie. Tyler said it was good."

"Sara went the other night with Dylan. She said it was really good. And I forgot, she invited us to go to Matt's on Saturday night. You think y'all can make it?"

"I don't know. Maybe."

"Come on, Sunny. I really don't want to be there

with just them. It'll be more fun if you two come. I think Dylan and Macy are coming, too."

When she looked over at Katelyn and saw the pleading look on her face, she knew she'd never be able to tell her no. With a disappointed groan, she told her, "Okay. I'll ask him about it."

"Awesome. We'll have such a blast."

"I haven't asked him yet," Sunny scoffed.

Sounding overly dramatic, Katelyn teased, "Like he'd ever tell you *no*. *He loves you.*"

"You are such a pain."

"I know, but you love me."

Sunny dropped off Katelyn at her parent's place and then headed back to the clubhouse. She sent Gavin a text letting him know that she was back, then went to her room to get dressed. She'd just finished putting on her boots when there was a knock on her door. "Coming!"

When she opened the door, she found Gavin standing there in his leather jacket and a dark t-shirt clinging to his defined chest. She'd always found him to be attractive—more than attractive. He was one of the hottest guys she'd ever seen, especially when those dark green eyes were aimed at her, just like they were now. She let out a silent sigh as she tried to gather her senses and took a step back to let him in. Gavin smiled at her reaction. He liked that he got to her the way he did. He loved watching the light blush of pink creep across her face whenever he got close to her. After all this time, she still hadn't realized he felt the same way about her. She completely captivated him, and he'd make any excuse just to see her.

He stepped towards her and smiled. "You ready?"

"Umm... yeah... but, I thought we weren't going for another hour."

"Got a stop to make before we head to dinner."

"Okay. Just let me grab my purse."

Over the past couple of weeks, Sunny and Gavin had spent all their free time together doing what most new couples do: eating out, movies, bowling, and going to clubs. They always had a great time, but they enjoyed their quiet times alone the most. There was nothing better than curling up in Sunny's bed. With the kitten nestled at their feet, they'd slip under the covers and watch a movie together. They'd spend the night talking and kissing, and in that room, it was as if they were the only two people in the world.

Sunny followed Gavin to the parking lot to his Jeep. Once he helped her inside, he started the engine and headed towards town. A small grin crossed her face when she noticed that he was wearing her favorite cologne. She inhaled deeply, settled into her seat, and stared out the window. Winter was setting in. The leaves had fallen off the trees, and the winter wheat was growing in the fields. She was focused on the scenery when she realized that Gavin was being oddly quiet as he drove downtown. She looked at him and became worried when she saw how tightly he was holding the steering wheel and the stressed look on his face. With each turn, he seemed to get more and more anxious, and Sunny couldn't figure out why.

"Is something wrong?"

"No. Everything's fine."

The stiffness in his back told her that he wasn't being completely honest with her. "You don't seem like everything's fine. Something is definitely on your mind."

He pulled the Jeep into an apartment complex and drove to the middle of the parking lot, then parked next to a motorcycle. "Got something for you to see."

Sunny looked over at the bike and quickly noticed the familiar dark burgundy paint and the Devil Chaser's logo on the back fender. With a puzzled look on her face, she asked, "What is Bishop doing here?"

"He told me to bring you by."

"Gavin," she scolded. "What is going on?"

He placed his hand on hers and said, "Just trust me. You'll know everything in just a few minutes."

"Okay." She got out of the Jeep and followed him up the stairs. Gavin knocked on one of the apartment doors. Seconds later, Bishop answered.

He took a step back, making way for Sunny and Gavin to enter. "Come check it out. He picked out a good one." Sunny stepped inside the apartment, and she was surprised how big it was. It had an open concept with a large living room that connected to the kitchen. There was a brand new tan sofa with end tables and a coffee table. She continued farther inside and saw that it had a new kitchen with a round table and chairs and all the latest appliances. The décor was simple, but she loved it.

As she continued to look around, Bishop explained, "Bobby installed a top of the line security system. It's synced to your cell phone and mine. If there is any problem, we will know. There are two bedrooms, so you and Katelyn will have plenty of room. She is waiting for you to decide which one you'd like to have."

"Wait. I don't understand." Sunny stopped and took a step over to Bishop, looking at him with utter confusion. "What is all this?"

"It's been a year, Lucky. We thought it was time for you to have a place of your own."

"You want me to leave the clubhouse?" Sunny asked. She began to wonder if she'd overstayed her welcome, fearing that the guys had become tired of watching over her. She hated to think that they were wanting her to leave and found herself trying to fight back her tears.

He placed his hands on her shoulders and said, "No. That's not it at all. The clubhouse is always open to you. The guys like having you there. You know that."

"Then what is all this?"

"Like I said… It's time for you to have a place of your own."

"What about Drew? What if he…"

"Don't. This isn't a time for what-ifs. You have to find a way to put the past behind you, for good. You've gotta stop hiding behind the walls of that clubhouse. You've got a bright future ahead of you." Bishop looked over to Gavin and paused a moment before he continued, "Only you can decide when you are ready to start living again, Sunny. The apartment is yours when you do."

She took a step back, looking at her new place, and a tightness filled her chest. Everything she'd always wanted was within her grasp, but she had to find the strength to reach out and grab it.

Sensing her struggle, Gavin walked up behind her and wrapped his arms around her waist. "You've got this, baby. You just have to take that first step."

"It's really a great place."

Bishop smiled. "It's not going anywhere. Take your time, and when you get ready, it will be here waiting."

"And Katelyn is moving in?"

"She and Gavin have been getting things set up for the past week."

"I can't believe she hasn't said anything," Sunny said with surprise.

"It wasn't easy. She was pretty excited about it." Gavin laughed. "I thought she'd spill the news for sure."

Sunny looked over at him. "Was this your idea?"

With a slight nod, he'd given her his answer. "Figured it was time for you to have a fresh start."

"Thank you." She eased up on her tiptoes and gave him a quick kiss. "I love it."

"Want to see the rest?" Gavin asked.

"Sure."

She followed him to the back and as she stepped into her new bedroom, she heard Katelyn ask, "Are they here?"

"Back here, Katelyn."

Katelyn started walking towards the bedrooms and found Sunny waiting for her in the hall. Normally, she knew right away what kind of mood Sunny was in, but at that moment, she had no idea what her friend was thinking. "What do you think?"

"I think it's amazing. I just can't believe you kept this all a secret."

"Gavin wanted to surprise you."

"I'm definitely surprised."

Katelyn could see that Sunny was having her doubts, so she slipped her arm through hers and pulled her into Sunny's new bedroom. "We've always talked about getting a place together, and this place is so cool."

"You really think I can do this?"

Katelyn gave her a tight hug and answered, "Absolutely. This is going to be awesome."

"Okay, then I guess we're roommates!"

"That's what I'm talking about." Katelyn gave her a tight hug. "I've gotta get to work before my boss blows a gasket, but I'll be back tomorrow to help you get your stuff packed."

"Sounds good." Sunny followed her back into the living room. When she saw that Bishop was about to leave, she walked over to him and said, "Thank you for all of this."

"No need to thank me." He looked over at Gavin. "This was all him."

Once Katelyn and Bishop were gone, Sunny took some time looking around the apartment, opening cabinet doors and peeking in closets while Gavin waited patiently on the sofa. He tried to make himself busy by looking over his emails and checking the weather on his phone, but he couldn't take his eyes off her. He loved watching her wander around the apartment and seeing how excited she was becoming. When she stepped out of the kitchen, there was a wild look in her eye. He wasn't sure what she was thinking until she started to race over to him. She pounced into his lap and put her knees at his sides, straddling his waist as she leaned down and kissed him.

Her eyes danced with excitement as she told him, "I love it. I really, really do."

"Glad to hear that. I was hoping you would."

"Well, I do. Very much," she told him as she lowered her mouth to his, kissing him tenderly. His hand reached to the back of her neck, tangling in her hair as he took control of the kiss. It quickly became heated, and Gavin couldn't hide how much he wanted her. When Sunny felt his thickness beneath her, she eagerly reached for the hem of his t-shirt and pulled it over his head, then removed her own and tossed it to the floor. The tips of his fingers trailed along her skin as he reached for her bra, gently slipping it down her shoulders. His kisses followed his touch as he pulled her breast free, lightly caressing it in his hand. Her head fell back as he began to nip and suck at her sensitive flesh, sending jolts of pleasure coursing through her body as he took her nipple into his mouth.

The warmth of his breath caressed her skin when he growled, "You're mine."

"Yes," she panted as she rocked her hips against him. Impatience overcame her as she lowered her hand between them, sliding it slowly between his legs. He immediately reached for her waist as he stood up from the sofa and carried her into her new bedroom. He lowered her down onto the bare mattress, and with a mischievous smile, he began to unbutton his jeans and lowered them to the floor. With him watching, Sunny slowly began inching her jeans and panties down her hips. She'd barely gotten them off when he dropped to the bed and settled himself between her legs. With her knees at his side, a low growl vibrated through his chest as his erection brushed against her center. He looked down at her, his eyes roaming appraisingly over her naked body, and she started to writhe under the heat of his gaze. His hands slowly snaked over her hips and up to her breasts, squeezing them gently in the palm of his hands. She wrapped her legs around his hips and pulled him closer as she brushed against the head of his cock.

"Fuck," he groaned as he dug his fingers into her flesh.

His mouth crashed down on hers, and his hand instinctively reached for the back of her neck, grasping at the hair around the nape of her neck as he deepened the kiss. His touch set her on fire. Every inch of her body burned for more, making the anticipation of having him inside her almost too much to bear. She looked up at him and pleaded, "Gavin."

She could see the emotion that crossed his face when he looked at her and said, "Never dreamed it'd feel like this."

Her eyes locked with his as she replied, "I know. You make me feel whole again."

"I love you, Sunny Jacobs."

She had no doubt he meant every word.

She looked down at him and saw the love in his eyes as she said, "I love you too, Gavin. More than I ever thought possible."

Chapter 11

"How did you fit all this stuff in that one little room?" Bull asked as he carried another large box out to the truck.

"My lucky girl's going to need a bigger closet," Gavin scoffed as he passed by him in the hall. They'd been helping Sunny move over to her new apartment all morning, and there was still lots left to move. Gavin was clearly eager to get done as he whipped past her with another load of boxes and bags towering in his arms.

Trying her best to ignore the wobbling boxes in Gavin's hands, Sunny followed behind Bull with her duffle bag full of shoes. "I'm beginning to think I'm a packrat. I didn't realize I had so many clothes. It's kind of ridiculous."

"It's not that bad. I've seen worse," Bull told her as they walked outside and over to the truck.

"Oh yeah? Sounds like there's a story behind that."

He pushed the cardboard box into the back of the truck and then turned and reached for Sunny's duffle bag. Once he'd put it away, he said, "Some stories aren't worth the breath it takes to tell 'em."

"Maybe, but I'd still like to hear it."

He started walking back inside, and with his back to her, he said, "I was a stupid kid. Thought I'd found the one. All I found was a whole lot of heartache and a shit-ton of unpaid bills."

"Oh."

"She was a real beauty. Don't think I'll ever forget that smile of hers."

There was a sadness in his voice that tugged at Sunny's heart. "Sounds like you loved her."

"I did. Loved her like I'd never loved anyone, and then one day she was gone. Packed one bag and left the rest of her shit behind."

When they got back to Sunny's room, Gavin had already filled his arms full of boxes and was walking out of the room. He smiled at Sunny as he said, "Just a few more and we'll be done."

Once he walked out, Sunny and Bull grabbed another box and quickly followed behind him. Before they stepped back outside, Sunny asked, "Did you ever try and find her?"

"I did, but after a while, I figured I was just wastin' my time."

"But didn't you wonder if something happened to her? Like something bad might have happened?"

"No. I knew why she'd left."

"Why?"

"Another guy. Had more money than you could shake a stick at. She knew I couldn't give her what he could, so she left. Can't say I blame her, but it was a real bitch moving all her shit out of my place."

"If that's the real reason she left, then she's an idiot. You're a catch, Bull, and you're better off without a woman like that."

"Yeah, you're probably right about that, but I sure loved that woman's cornbread. Some of the best I ever had." He laughed as he put their boxes in the back of the truck.

"Cornbread? Bull, you are a nut!"

"No doubt about that. Now, enough about me and my shit. How 'bout you? You good?"

"I think so... I've started having those dreams again."

"About that night?"

"Yes. The same stupid dream. They seem so real, like I'm right back there. I get to the same point each time, and then it just stops and starts all over again. It's like I'm trapped in some weird cycle. You'd think by now, it would've gotten better."

"You just need time. They'll stop."

"It's like my mind is trying to get me to remember something. The memory is right there, but I just can't get to it."

"Maybe it's best that you don't."

"How am I supposed to get over my past if I can't even remember it?"

"There's nothing you can do to change things, so just leave it where it belongs... in the past. Focus on the future."

"I guess you're right."

"I usually am," he laughed.

They were standing by the truck talking when Gavin walked out with the last of the boxes balancing in his arms. "Are you two gonna help me or what?"

They both rushed over and helped Gavin get the rest of her things packed into the truck. Once they were finished, Sunny told them, "I really appreciate you guys helping me. Lunch is on me."

Bull patted his abdomen as he said, "Deal. I'm starving."

"Wait." Gavin looked over to Sunny. "What about Scout?"

"Already got her in the truck."

"And her food and litter?"

"Got it."

"Then, we're set. Let's roll," Gavin told them.

By the time they had everything moved over to the apartment, Katelyn had gotten off work and helped Sunny unpack, while Gavin went to the garage to get caught up with work. It took most of the night, but the girls finally got everything set up just the way they wanted it. Sunny sat down on the sofa and looked around, seeing parts of herself scattered around the room. Those anxious feelings that she'd had about moving were gone. For the first time, she had a place of her own and found herself feeling hopeful about all the new possibilities. She reached for her new college schedule, and even though they didn't start for several more weeks, she was excited about all the new classes she would be taking. After talking to Ana, she'd decided to make nursing her major. It had always been something she'd considered but never thought she'd have the means to do it. Now that she had her chance, she would do whatever it took to see it through. She was determined to stop letting her fears about Drew control her, and she would put her calculated life in the past. The future was there waiting for her, and she was ready to take that first step forward.

When she noticed how late it was, she reached for her phone and sent a text message to Gavin.

Sunny:

I thought you were coming by.

Gavin:

About to head that way. You okay?

Sunny:

I'm great. Just missing you.

Gavin:

Give me ten minutes. Want me to bring dinner?

Sunny:

Yes! I'm starving.

Gavin:

What about Katelyn?

Sunny turned her head towards Katelyn's room and shouted, "Do you want anything to eat? Gavin is bringing takeout."

She came out of her room wearing a pair of jeans and her favorite red sweater. Her hair was all fixed and she'd put on makeup. "No, thanks. I've got plans."

"I can see that. Where are you headed?"

"Just going out for a bit. I won't be long."

"So, it's a secret?"

"No. I'm just going out." She grabbed her purse and keys as she started for the door. "Call me if you need me."

"Okay. Be careful."

"You know I will." She smiled and closed the door behind her.

Sunny looked back down at her phone and responded:

Sunny:

It's just us.

Gavin:

Okay. Be there soon.

She looked back over at the door and curiosity washed over her. It wasn't like Katelyn to keep things from her. They'd never kept secrets, which made her wonder why she hadn't said anything about her plans. She couldn't help but wonder if it had something to do with Conner and Levi. Before she could think too much about it, there was a tapping noise outside her door. Thinking it was Gavin, she hopped up and opened the door, only to find no one there. She was about to shut the door when she spotted a small white envelope sitting on their welcome mat. Without thinking too much about it, she reached for it and went back inside, locking the door behind her. There was no name written on the outside, and she started to wonder if the mysterious note must have had something to do with Katelyn and her odd behavior. She was just about to open it when there was another knock at the door.

She placed the envelope on the counter. "Who is it?"

"It's me," Gavin answered.

This time when she opened the door, she found Gavin standing behind it with a big smile and an armful of Chinese takeout. "What is all that? I said it was just us."

As soon as he stepped inside, the kitten pranced over to him, weaving between his feet. "Hey there, Scout." He placed the large brown paper bag on the kitchen table and reached down to pick up the kitten, scratching the top of her head. "You said you were starving."

"I did, but this is enough food for an army."

"It's Chinese. We'll eat, and in an hour, we'll be hungry again." He lowered the kitten to the floor and started to unpack the sack full of food.

"True. I guess you've got us covered, then," she laughed.

"That I do. Now, get your cute ass over here and eat."

They both fixed themselves a plate and once they were done eating, Gavin stood up and started cleaning their mess. Sunny looked at all the leftovers and laughed. "We definitely have plenty for later."

He reached for her plate and said, "That's the plan."

Sunny followed him into the kitchen and helped him put everything away. They'd just about finished when Gavin noticed the envelope. He picked it up and turned to Sunny as he asked, "Is this trash, too?"

"I don't know what that is. I think it's for Katelyn, or else it's something she dropped on her way out." She placed the leftovers in the fridge and closed the door before she started back into the living room. "It was on the front mat."

Something didn't feel right as Gavin studied the small white envelope. He held it up to the light hoping he'd be able to see what was written inside, but he didn't have any luck. A gnawing feeling started to build in his gut, and he was just about to ask her to open it when she called out, "Open it if you want to."

He quickly tore it open, and his chest tightened when he read what was written inside:

I saw what you did.
Meet me at Paris Landing Lodge on Sunday at 10 a.m.
or I go to the police.

He reached for his phone and took a picture of the note, then sent it to Bishop with a message:

Gavin:

We've got a problem.

Bishop:

Who's it from?

Gavin:

No idea. Someone left it on Sunny's mat. Have Bobby check the security feed.

Gavin folded the note and shoved it into his back pocket as he walked back into the living room. "It's just a bill from the landlord. I'll get it to Bishop."

"What kind of bill?"

"Some upgrades Bishop had done before you guys moved. He's been expecting it. Nothing for you to worry about," he told her as his phone chimed with a text message. He looked down at the screen to see what Bishop had replied.

Bishop:

On it. Don't tell her what's going on. Just find an excuse to get her back to the clubhouse.

Gavin:

Be there in 10.

"Okay." She picked up the remote and asked, "Wanna watch a movie?"

"Got something I need to take care of."

"Oh," she answered with disappointment.

"You're going with me."

With a puzzled look on her face, she turned to him and asked, "I am?"

"Text Katelyn and let her know you won't be back tonight."

There was something about his tone that worried Sunny. The playfulness he had during dinner was gone and replaced with apprehension. She could see that he was worried about something, so she asked, "Is something wrong?"

He held up his phone to her as he explained, "That was Bishop. I need to get over to the clubhouse to see him before he leaves for the night. Figured we'd just stay there since it was late."

"Okay." Sunny got up off the sofa and slipped on her boots before heading towards the door. "Then let's go."

Once they got into his Jeep and started towards the clubhouse, Sunny became even more worried. Neither of them spoke as Gavin drove. She saw how tightly he gripped the steering wheel and knew without a doubt something was wrong. When they made it through the gate, Gavin turned to her and said, "I won't be long. Just wait for me in my room until I get done."

She opened the door to the Jeep and nodded. She wanted to ask him again if something was wrong, but knew he wouldn't tell her. She'd been around long enough to know that this is how it was with brothers of the club; they kept things on a need-to-know basis, and if Gavin thought she should know what was going on, he'd tell her. She'd just have to trust him, so she went to his room and tried her best to ignore the anxious feeling that kept churning inside her. Just as she was curling up in his bed, Gavin was about to walk into Bishop's office.

When he opened the door, he heard Bobby say, "Things are finally coming together in Mexico. Think we've finally got our guy. I should have everything set by the end of the night."

"That's good news. We'll finally be able to put this thing to rest. Let me know how it plays out."

He was too concerned about Sunny to ask what they were talking about. Instead, he continued inside the office and sat down beside Bobby while Bishop sat in front of him, sifting through several papers. "Any idea who left the note?"

Bishop passed the papers over to Gavin and said, "Melissa Reynolds. Bobby got her license plate number when she pulled out of the apartment complex."

"And who the hell is Melissa Reynolds?"

"Drew's neighbor," Bobby answered. "He was screwing around with her when he was dating Sunny."

"She found out he was fucking around and dumped his sorry ass," Bishop added.

"So, what the hell does she want?"

"Not sure, but we'll take care of it," Bishop assured him.

"Do you really think she saw something? Do you think…" Gavin started.

"Doesn't matter what she did or didn't see. We'll take care of it. You look after Sunny. Do what you can to keep things as normal as possible, and I'll handle the rest."

"She's made plans for us to go out tomorrow night."

"Then take her," Bishop ordered. "Just make sure Bull and Otis are there to keep an eye on things."

As he stood to leave, Gavin turned to Bobby and said, "It's been a fucking year. Any idea why she'd try to contact Sunny now?"

"That's what we plan to find out. I'll keep digging. If there's anything to know, I'll find it."

"You'll know as soon as we do," Bishop assured him.

Gavin nodded, and before he walked out the door, he turned to Bishop. "I love her, brother."

"We all do. You gotta know we'll do whatever it takes to keep her safe."

"Good." Gavin looked him in the eye. "I'm gonna hold you to that."

Chapter 12

Sunny looked at herself in the mirror, checking her hair and makeup one last time before joining the others. Since it was getting colder, she'd opted to wear her black V-neck sweater with skinny jeans and boots. Her hair was done with long, loose curls that cascaded down her shoulders, and she'd done her best to do her makeup the way Katelyn had done it a few weeks earlier. Once she'd put on a hint of perfume, she headed to the living room. When she walked in, Gavin was on the sofa with the kitten curled up in his lap. He was fiddling with his phone while Katelyn was at the table putting on her favorite pair of slutty high heel boots.

Sunny smiled as she said, "So, it's going to be one of those nights?"

Katelyn stood and adjusted her short skirt. "I don't know what you're talking about."

"Mm-hmm," she scoffed. Sunny walked over to Gavin and asked, "Are you ready to head out?"

Without looking up from his phone, he answered, "Whenever you are."

She'd hoped that his talk with Bishop would've made him better, but it hadn't. In fact, it'd only made him worse. He was quiet and withdrawn. He hadn't talked to her, much less looked at her, and she was desperate to pull him out of his fog. Thinking she could goad him out of it, she sassed, "You know... you can just stay here if you don't want to go. I'm sure I can round up some hot guys that would be happy to entertain me for the night."

She immediately regretted her comment when Gavin looked up at her with his eyebrow raised and a mischievous spark in his eye. He moved the kitten over to the sofa and slowly started to stand. He took a step towards her as he asked, "Oh, yeah?"

She stumbled back and laughed. "*Gavin...* I was just playing around. You know I didn't mean it."

He reached for her and pulled her over to him. His mouth dropped to her ear and the heat of his breath sent chills down her spine as he whispered, "Mine."

She giggled as her arms wound around his neck. "You're such a caveman."

"Do I need to bring my club to Matt's?"

"I think you're good without it," she told him as she lifted up on her tiptoes and gave him a kiss.

He looked down at her, admiring her outfit as he said, "Liking the getup. Looks good on you, but it's gonna look even better on the floor later tonight."

"I'm looking forward to that."

"Not as much as I am," he told her just before he kissed her once again. "You really do look beautiful."

"Thank you. Not looking so bad yourself." While others might find his look intimidating, she'd always loved how he looked in his leather jacket and jeans. His tattoos were hidden beneath his clothes, but she knew they were there. She'd seen them every time they'd made love, and just knowing they were there made her look forward to watching him undress later that night. As soon as the thought crossed her mind, Gavin noticed. There was no hiding the lust in her eyes, and he wanted nothing more than to skip going to the club and spend the entire night locked away in her room buried deep inside her.

He was just about to kiss her again when Katelyn cleared her throat in an obvious attempt to distract them. "Can we go before you two make me gag?" Katelyn shook her head as she grabbed her purse.

Sunny laughed as she patted Gavin on the chest. "Let's go, Caveman."

"If we must," he told her as he reached for Sunny's hand. With Katelyn following behind, Gavin led her out to his Jeep. Before he pulled out of the parking lot, he sent Bull a text message letting him know they were on their way. As soon as he started the engine, the girls started talking and didn't stop until he pulled up to the bar. He had no idea what they were talking about. It didn't matter. All he cared about was seeing that smile on Sunny's face. He'd do anything to keep it there, including spending a night at Matt's pub with Katelyn's crazy friend Sara. He parked the Jeep, and before Sunny opened her door, he reached for her. "Wait. I'll come around."

As soon as he stepped out of the Jeep, the bar's loud music echoed around him. Ignoring the loud, thumping bass, he scanned the parking lot and quickly noticed Otis's bike parked close to the front door next to Bull's. Feeling relieved to know they were there, he continued over to her side of the Jeep. When he opened her door, Sunny stepped out and waited for Katelyn to do the same. She ran her fingers through her short blonde hair and gave it a quick fluff. With an exaggerated sway to her hips, she headed towards the door. "Come on, guys. Let's do this."

Sunny and Gavin followed her into the crowded bar and over to one of the empty tables in the back. Once the girls were settled, Gavin went to the bar to get them a drink. He'd just made it back to the table when Sara stumbled over to them. Her dark hair was pulled up in a messy bun with loose curls falling around her face. She was wearing a short black skirt, too short for her own good, and a pair of red six-inch heels. It was obvious that she'd already been drinking when she tried to keep her balance by placing the palm of her hand on the table. She leaned towards them and slurred her words as she shouted, "Hey, bitches. Where the hell have you been?"

Katelyn rolled her eyes as she said, "It's not even ten, Sara. How can you already be wasted?"

She tried to stand upright, but wobbled as she

scoffed, "I'm not wasted. I'm just getting started. This is my favorite song! Come on, let's get out there and dance."

Katelyn took a long sip of her drink before she stood and asked, "Where's Dylan and Macy?"

"Girl, I left Dylan at home. He's been in a bad mood all week, and I'm tired of his sorry ass bringing me down. And Macy should be here any minute."

Before she left, Katelyn looked over to Sunny and asked, "You coming?"

"Y'all go ahead. I'll be out there in a minute."

Sunny watched as her friends headed out onto the dance floor. In a matter of seconds, they were surrounded by a group of horny guys, but neither of them seemed to care. They were too busy laughing and dancing to even notice how they were gawking at them. When she looked around the room, she spotted Bull and Otis sitting across the room and waved to them, trying to get their attention. She turned to Gavin and asked, "Did you know Bull and Otis were here?"

"Saw their bikes out front."

"You should get them to come over and have a drink with us."

"Maybe later," he told her just as the DJ put on a slow song. He stood up and reached for her hand. "Right now, I want to dance with my girl."

Hoping a dance might distract her from his brothers in the corner, he led her through the crowd and over to

Katelyn where she was dancing with some random guy. Gavin wrapped his arms around her, pulling her close as they started to sway to the rhythm of the music. Sunny loved being in his arms, smelling the scent of his cologne and the warmth of his body next to hers, and it didn't take her long to get lost in the moment. She rested her head on his shoulder as she listened to the words of the song. They'd been dancing for several minutes when Sunny's attention was drawn over to Bull's table. Levi and Conner were now sitting with them, and both had their eyes set on Katelyn. They watched her every move as she sashayed across the dance floor, laughing and singing.

The song ended and Katelyn left her dancing partner and headed over to Gavin and Sunny. "I need a drink."

They all started back over to the table, but stopped when someone called out, "Katie!"

They all turned and anger flashed over Katelyn's face when she saw Justin walking in their direction. "What are you doing here, Justin?"

"Sara mentioned that you were coming tonight. She told me to come. She knew I wanted a chance to talk to you."

"I've got nothing to say to you. Seriously, it's over."

Sunny looked over to Justin and said, "Hey, Justin."

"Hey there, Sunshine."

An odd sensation swept over Sunny when she heard her ex-boyfriend's pet name for her. She hadn't heard it since the night of the attack, and it was one of the pieces of the puzzle she'd been missing. Trying to ignore the anxious feeling she felt stirring in the pit of her stomach, she said, "Sara shouldn't have told you to come. Maybe you should just go."

"No 'maybe' about it. You should go. No one wants you here," Katelyn snapped.

"Why do you have to be like that? I told you I was sorry."

"And I told you I didn't care that you were sorry."

Katelyn turned to leave, but Justin reached for her arm and tugged her back over to him. Before he had a chance to speak, Gavin stepped between them, breaking Katelyn free from his grip. "It's time for you to go."

"Who the fuck are you?" he snarled. "You fucking her now?"

Gavin took a step towards him and growled, "You've got two choices, asshole. You can either turn around and walk the fuck out of here while you still can, or they can carry your sorry ass out on a stretcher."

"Justin," Sunny pleaded.

He released his grip on Katelyn's arm as he spat, "Forget it. She's nothing but a two-bit whore. You can have her."

He'd barely gotten the words out of his mouth when Conner and Levi came crashing through the crowd. With one punch, Conner laid him out on the floor. Justin brought his hand up to the side of his face as he groaned, "What the fuck?"

Katelyn's eyes widened with shock as she looked over to Conner and Levi and asked, "What are you guys doing here?"

Levi grabbed the back of Justin's collar and started pulling him towards the front door. Justin tried to wiggle free from his grasp, but it was useless. "Let me fucking go!"

"Levi!" Katelyn shouted. "Let him go. He's not worth it."

She knew Justin was just upset and didn't mean what he'd said. He'd never do anything to hurt her, at least not intentionally. But no one seemed to listen. Conner and Gavin walked past her as they followed Levi out into the parking lot. She stood there dazed for a moment, then like she'd been stung by a bee, she quickly scurried. Against her better judgement, Sunny followed Katelyn out into the parking lot. They both watched as the guys hauled Justin over to his truck. The sound of his feet raking over the gravel triggered something deep inside of Sunny, causing her to stop dead in her tracks. She watched in a daze as Conner pulled Justin to his feet and placed his hand around his throat, squeezing tightly as he threatened him. She'd never know exactly what caused it, but in that moment, everything around her stood still.

Sunshine.

His callous voice echoing in the back of her mind.

Sunshine.

Nausea washed over her as the memories started rushing back to her, one by one. The words that haunted her dreams bombarded her all at once.

"Hey there, Sunshine. Where ya headed in such a rush?"

"A bunch of drunks pawing over what's mine."

"I fucking loved you!"

Her knees grew weak as she stood there watching Conner with Justin. Hearing the anger in his voice. The chill of the night nipping at her skin. It was coming back to her. Each memory more vivid than the last.

His hand twisting deep in her hair.

The smell of beer on his breath before he slammed the bottle against her head, and the feel of the cold liquid splashing across her chest as the bottle broke.

The pain she felt when he kicked her over and over again.

These memories were not new to her. She'd seen them in her dreams, but now there was more. She could see the night unfolding before her. Her chest tightened as she remembered him dragging her lifeless body across the empty parking lot. The feel of the rocks grinding into her back. The angry curses he mumbled as he yanked her forward. Her body was broken and bruised. Several of her ribs cracked from all the vicious kicks from his boots. She could hardly take a breath as her head pounded aimlessly against the gravel. Her eyes were almost swollen shut, but she could see his truck was just a few feet away. Her end was drawing near. She could feel it in her bones. When he finally reached the truck, he released her hands and opened the tailgate.

Adrenaline surged through her as her hands fumbled across the loose gravel. She knew she had to find something, some way to defend herself, before he killed her. A feeling of hope rushed over her when the tips of her fingers brushed across one large, pointy rock. She tried with all her might to reach for it, but it was just out of her grasp. Her heart sank when she was lifted from the ground and her back slammed against the bed of the truck. Everything fell silent. She tried to listen, to concentrate, but heard nothing. She had no idea what he was doing until she felt him tug at the waistband of her jeans.

"No!" she shouted, but the word never made it out of her mouth. Not that it mattered. No one was there to hear her as he jerked the jeans down her hips. She could shout from the rooftop, but there would be no one to come to her rescue. She was completely alone, and it was up to her to either save herself or die. He started working on his own pants, and with his attention diverted, she sprawled out her hands and searched for something that might help. She was about to give up hope when she felt an old rusted tire iron. Taking it firmly in her hand, she waited for him to come close enough for her to strike him. She didn't have to wait long. He placed his grubby hands on her hips as he tugged her bare body towards him, and he never saw it coming. She lifted the tire iron and slammed it against the side of his head. His limp body immediately dropped to her side. Still rattled with fear, Sunny managed to raise herself up, lifting the tire iron in her hand, and hit him again.

And again.

And again.

She couldn't remember how many times she'd struck him, but she remembered the blood and how the sticky wetness clung to her fingers. A loud clatter echoed around her when she dropped the tire iron onto the bed of the truck, and then everything fell silent. When she tried to move, her body refused. Every muscle in her body screamed at her to stop, and when she couldn't stand the pain a moment longer, she eased back, resting her head on the cold metal of the truck. Everything around her blurred, and then it was over.

She remembered.

With tears streaming down her face, she stumbled back and fell down onto the gravel. She drew her knees up to her chest and started to sob. "Oh my god."

Katelyn knelt in front of her. "Sunny? What's wrong?" She put her hand on Sunny's shoulder trying to get through to her, but Sunny just continued to cry uncontrollably. Her breaths became short and strained, like she was about to hyperventilate. Katelyn turned towards the guys and yelled, "Gavin! Something's wrong with Sunny!"

When he turned and saw them huddled together on the ground, he rushed over to Sunny and placed his hands on the side of her face. Gently lifting her head, he forced her to look at him as he asked, "Sunny? What's wrong? Are you hurt?"

"Gavin." Pain and fear filled her eyes as she cried, "Did I kill him?"

Looking completely confused, Katelyn turned to Gavin and asked, "What the hell is she talking about? Kill who?"

Ignoring Katelyn, he quickly lifted Sunny into his arms, cradling her close to his chest as he took her over to the Jeep. He opened her door, and once they were both settled inside, she muttered, "What did I do? What did I do?"

"Just breathe, Sunny." Her face was wet with tears, and his heart broke to see her so distraught. As much as he'd hoped it never would, the past had found its way back into the present. He wanted to make it all go away, to find a way to erase everything that had happened, but there was nothing he could do.

"He was going to rape me," she sobbed, her chest heaving up and down as she tried to take in a breath. "I hit him. There was blood... so much blood. Oh god.

What did I do?"

"Sunny, it's going to be okay… I need you to try to calm down."

"It happened so fast. I didn't know what else to do. I was so scared. He was going to kill me… I just wanted to make him stop."

"You did what you had to do," he told her as he started the engine. "I'm taking you back to the clubhouse."

She looked over to him, and with her voice trembling, she said, "I need to know what happened. I need to know everything."

"You'll get the answers you need, but for now, I need to you try to hold it together."

And she did try, but that didn't stop the tears from flowing down her face. Sunny was too upset to put all the pieces of the puzzle together, but Gavin knew she eventually would. He knew it would be hard for her to accept, but in time, she'd understand. He looked over at her, and a feeling of helplessness came over him. He wanted to explain everything to her, to tell her exactly how it all played out, but he couldn't. He'd given his word, and until Bishop gave the okay, he would have to remain silent. Sunny continued to cry as he drove out onto the highway, and by the time he'd gotten back to the clubhouse, she was a wreck. Once he'd parked the Jeep, he pulled his phone out of his pocket and sent a message to Bishop.

The Long Road Home

Gavin:

She remembered.

He quickly shoved it back in his pocket and turned to Sunny. He reached for her hand, pulling her over to him, and said, "From the very first day I saw you, I knew there was something special about you. I'm not the only one who can see it. Everyone can. There's a fire burning inside of you, and its light shines from within. It's who you are—who you are meant to be. Remember that. Hold onto it. Fight for it. You're the only one who can."

His words calmed her racing heart, but it didn't stop the ache that was lodged deep inside her. The memory of what she'd gone through and what she'd done tore at her, ripping at her very soul. In her mind, she knew she had killed Drew in self-defense. He hadn't left her any choice, but the fact still remained, she killed him. There were so many unanswered questions, so many secrets left to be revealed, leaving her feeling lost and confused. She wanted to know, needed to know, but she was too far gone to even ask. Those questions would have to wait. For now, she opened the door to the Jeep and said, "I can't. I just can't."

Sunny got out and started walking towards her car. He rushed after her and asked, "Where are you going?"

"I need some time alone, Gavin. I need time to

think."

"That's the last thing you need right now."

"What happened after I passed out? Did I kill him? Is Drew dead?" Sunny pushed.

The tightness in her chest grew stronger, making it difficult for her to breathe as the panic started to rise within her. "Where is he?" He didn't answer, but she could tell by the expression on his face that he knew. He knew everything, and he'd known it all along. "Dammit, Gavin. How could you keep that from me? You know what I've gone through over the last year."

"I didn't have a choice."

"There's always a choice, Gavin." She'd had all she could take, and the need to escape overcame her. "I'm done with this right now. I can't take it anymore."

She stormed over to her car and as she opened her door, Gavin shouted, "Lucky, don't."

She looked over at him and snapped, "Don't call me that! Nothing about any of this is *Lucky*!"

"You're wrong. You've been lucky from the start. You just can't see that right now."

"*Please, just stop*! I can't stay here. I need to be alone.*"

Before Gavin had a chance to stop her, she started the car and drove out of the parking lot. She glanced back in her rearview mirror and tears trickled down her cheek as she saw Gavin standing there watching her leave. A feeling of regret washed over her as she drove out onto the highway. None of this was his fault, and she had no right to blame him. He'd been so good to her, loved her even when she was at her worst, and she lashed out at him instead of giving him a chance to explain. In her heart, she knew he didn't deserve for her to leave like she did, but she couldn't stay.

She had no destination in mind when she continued down the highway, but after just a few miles, the car seemed to know exactly where it was going. It was a place Sunny hadn't been in quite some time. During her darkest times, it had been a place where she'd once found solace, and if fate had its way, she'd be able to find it again.

Chapter 13

"She's fine," Bull assured Gavin. "She just showed up at her mother's place."

As soon as Sunny pulled through the gate, Gavin called Bobby and told him to use the tracker on her phone to find out where she was headed. After Bobby found her at the dock, Gavin sent Bull over to keep an eye on her.

"Is she there alone?"

"No. Glenda and Tyler are there with her."

"Good. I was hoping she'd end up there."

"You headed over to the meet?" Bull asked.

"We're headed over there now." He continued to follow Bishop down the highway toward the Paris Landing Lodge. Melissa would be expecting Sunny to be there, but she'd have to deal with them instead. "It's all falling apart."

"Nothing's falling apart, brother. It's just the opposite. Everything is finally coming together. Getting through this shit is the only way this thing is ever gonna be over. It's finally time for Sunny to face the past so she can move on. This is the only way that's ever gonna happen."

"Maybe you're right, but damn. It's a lot to take in."

"She's gonna be fine, Gavin. The girl is tough. Give her time and she'll sort through all of this."

"And I'll be here waiting when she does." He put his Jeep in park and killed the engine. Before he got out, he told him, "Let me know if she moves. We're headed inside."

"You got it. Good luck."

Gavin walked over to Bishop and watched as he reached into his saddlebag and pulled out a manila folder. Goliath came over to them and asked, "You ready?"

Bishop nodded and started towards the front door. Gavin followed them both into the main sitting area of the lodge. There weren't many people around this time of year, just a few fishermen and a couple of tourists, so it wouldn't be difficult for them to find Melissa. They walked past the large Christmas tree and over to the balcony. After a few seconds of searching, they found Melissa sitting in the corner by the fireplace. Gavin thought she looked much older than the girl that Bobby had shown him the night before, and he was surprised to see that she was holding her five-month-old daughter in her lap. Under the circumstances, he figured she would've left the baby at home. Her eyes widened with fear when she saw the three large men walking in her direction. She knew exactly who they were. She'd seen them many times before. Every time she'd tried to make contact with Sunny, one of them was always there. They were her guardians, and they'd already proven that there was nothing they wouldn't do to protect her.

The urge to run rushed through Melissa, but there was no escape; she'd brought this on, and now she'd have to deal with the fallout.

When they approached, she pulled her daughter close to her chest and said, "I don't want any trouble."

"You should've thought about that before you left that note on Sunny's doorstep," Bishop growled.

"It's not what you think." She looked down at her daughter and then back over to them. "I was desperate. I am desperate."

Bishop sat down next to her and calmly told her, "You're gonna have to give me more than that."

"It's hard to explain."

"Try," Bishop pushed.

"I had my reasons for leaving that note. I know I shouldn't have done it, but I didn't know what else to do."

"What reasons?" Goliath asked.

"I don't even know where to start," she mumbled. "When I started seeing Drew, I knew he was with Sunny, and I never thought things with us would ever go anywhere. We were just having a good time, but things changed after she broke it off with him. He started coming around more and wanted to make things work with us." She took a deep breath and then continued, "That's when everything went downhill. He became possessive and demanding. He'd lose his temper at the drop of a hat. One minute he would be the sweetest guy ever, and I loved being with him. Then some switch would flip inside of him, and he'd change into this vicious monster."

"What does any of this have to do with Sunny?" Gavin asked.

"I tried to break things off with him, but he just kept coming back. I couldn't get away from him. I was tired of him beating the hell out of me. I was tired of being afraid, and once I found out I was pregnant, I was scared that I'd never get away from him. I knew how crazy he was about her. I could hear it in his voice whenever he talked about her. I was hoping that he'd just go back to her, and I thought if he just saw her..." Tears started to fill her eyes when she said, "I never dreamed he'd hurt her."

"What did you do?" Gavin growled.

Her eyes dropped to the ground as she explained, "I told him about the bonfire. Told him that I'd heard Sunny and some of her friends were going after she got off work. Ten minutes after I told him, he was in his truck headed to find her. When I followed him, I was hoping to see them work things out. I didn't know it would play out like it did. I didn't know how bad it was until he started to pull her over to his truck."

"Why didn't you try to stop him?" Goliath asked her. "Or at least call for some fucking help?"

"I know I should've done something, but I panicked. I knew the whole thing was my fault. He would've never gone there if I'd kept my mouth shut, so I just waited and prayed that it would be okay. When I saw your truck coming down the road, I left. I didn't want to take the chance on you seeing me there."

Bishop motioned over to her daughter and asked, "Is that his kid?"

"Yes. She's the reason why I tried to contact Sunny. I know Sunny's been through hell, and I know it's all my fault. But my daughter," she cried, "she's so sick, and I didn't know what to do. No one even knows this is Drew's child. I couldn't tell his parents. I knew they'd never believe it was his, and I was doing okay until the doctors told me she had cancer. I lost my job because I've had to miss so much work. The treatments are working, but they're really expensive. I tried to think of some other way, but I was out of options."

"So you thought you could blackmail Sunny?"

Her voice trembled as she said, "It was stupid of me and I'm truly sorry, but you have to understand. I was desperate. Maddie's all I've got. But no matter what happened with me and Sunny, I would've never gone to the police. I knew she saved my life when she killed Drew. I could see how things were going. It was only a matter of time before he went too far."

Bishop handed her the folder and waited for her to look inside before he said, "You've got yourself a colorful past there. Petty theft. Drugs. Prostitution. The list goes on."

"That was a long time ago. I lost my way when my folks died, but I don't do that stuff anymore."

"Wouldn't take much to have DHS sniffing around your place, and with a past like this, they wouldn't think twice about taking your daughter away."

A look of terror crossed her face at the thought of losing her daughter. "No! Please... I won't say anything about that night. I'll leave here and you'll never hear from me again."

Bishop reached into the side pocket of his leather jacket and pulled out a thick envelope. "You fucked up, Melissa. You should've come to me from the start." He handed her the envelope. "Your daughter shouldn't have to pay for your mistake or her father's. This should cover her medical expenses for now."

"I don't know what to say."

"You don't say anything. Not one fucking word. We'll do what we can to help with the kid, but you keep your mouth shut and stay the hell away from Sunny. And know that we will be watching. The minute you even think about running your fucking mouth, you'll have hell waiting for you at your back door. I'll have child services on your ass, and that will be just the start. I'll do whatever it takes to ruin you. You have my word on that."

"I'll never say a word. I promise." She held the

envelope against her chest and started to sob. With tears streaming down her face, she kissed her daughter on the top of her head and said, "I can't thank you enough for this."

As he stood to leave, he told her, "My number is inside. If you need anything, let me know."

With that, they all turned and walked out of the lodge, leaving a relieved Melissa sitting in utter shock as she stared at the envelope full of cash. On the way out to the parking lot, Bishop asked Gavin, "Any word from Sunny?"

"She's with her mom."

"'Bout time for the two of us to have a talk." Bishop got on his bike and looked over at Gavin. "I know you're worried. We both know your girl's got a lot to sort through, but give her some time. It'll all play out like it's supposed to."

Gavin wanted to believe that he was right, but he was having his doubts. Sunny was shutting him out, and he feared that when everything was laid out and all the secrets were revealed, he might lose her for good. He couldn't stand the thought. He'd found his place with her. She was his home, his refuge, and the mere thought of having that ripped away terrified him. He prayed that in time she'd understand why things had to play out the way they did, and she'd find a way to move past it. He watched as Bishop drove out of the parking lot knowing that if anyone could get through to her, it would be him.

The Long Road Home

When Bishop pulled up to Glenda's house, Tyler was out front playing basketball. He got off his bike and walked over to him. "Your sister around?"

"I think she's out back," Tyler answered. "Something's wrong. She's been talking to Momma all morning, but they won't tell me what's going on."

"Mind if I go have a word with her?"

"You can try. I sure didn't have much luck."

"I'll see what I can do," Bishop told him. When he got to the backyard, he found Sunny sitting on the old tire swing bundled up in her jacket and winter gloves. He walked over to her and asked, "Got a minute?"

She looked up at him, her eyes puffy from crying, and said, "I don't think I'm ready for this conversation, Bishop."

He could see the doubt in her eyes as he took a step towards her. "It's been a long time coming."

"Will you be honest with me? No sugarcoating it?" she asked. There had been so many things kept from her, so many secrets, and she couldn't take it any longer. She needed to know it all, and she knew Bishop was the only one who could give her that.

"If that's the way you want it."

"Yes. That's the way I want it." She wiped a tear from the corner of her eye as she stood up from the swing and started walking towards Bishop's pond. When they stepped up onto the dock, Sunny turned to him and asked, "Did I kill Drew?"

"Yes. He was dead when I got there."

His words hit her like a punch to the gut. Deep in her heart, she already knew the answer, but there was still a part of her that held on to the hope that she was wrong.

She took a deep breath, trying to fight back her tears, and then forced herself to push forward. "What happened to him? Where's his body? And why didn't you tell the police? Why did you cover it all up? With his father and the police, how is this ever going to end? They're going to find out. They're going to eventually put it all together and come after me."

"Slow down, darlin'. Once I explain everything, then you'll understand why it played out like it did." He crossed his arms and leaned against the wooden rails as he looked over to her. He kept ahold of all of his emotions as he spoke, keeping his voice calm and soft. "Your mother called me that night. She got worried when you didn't answer her calls. I told her we'd go over to the bar and check on you. Gavin and Goliath were there when she called, so they came along."

"Gavin was there?"

"He was, and he was just as shocked as I was when we pulled into the parking lot and found you laid out in the back of that truck. You were in bad shape, Sunny. I thought we were going to lose you." He reached into his pocket for a cigarette and lit it before he continued. "We were going to call the sheriff. We all knew it was self-defense. That boy damn near killed you, but Sunny, it wasn't that simple... You reeked of beer, and with the number you did on him, we thought the cops might question your motive. I wasn't sure if you'd been drinking, but I couldn't take that chance. Not after what he'd done."

"What did you do?"

"We took care of it."

"You're not going to tell me what you did?" she pushed. There was no way he would ever tell her exactly what they'd done, but she'd hoped he'd give her something more, something that would help the storm of panic that was holding its grasp on her heart.

"He's gone. That's all you need to know."

"What about his truck? What about the cops?"

"Broken down for parts." Bishop took a step towards her. His eyes, intense and confident, locked on hers. "It's all been handled, and once Bobby puts his plan into place, it will all be over."

She shook her head. Without knowing what was really going on, she'd never be able to stop worrying that inevitably they would come after her. "And what is Bobby's plan?"

"It's something he's been working on for months. Just had to wait for the right scenario to play out, and the other night, it finally did. Soon, police will match his fingerprints to a John Doe in Mexico. Once that happens, the case will be closed, and you'll have nothing else to worry about."

"There's just so much," she told him with tears pooling in her eyes once again. "Why did you do all this?"

Bishop turned and ran his hand along the wooden rail of the dock and asked, "Did you know your dad helped me build this?"

Surprise crossed her face as she shook her head and waited for him to continue.

"Well, he did. He was a fine man... a good friend to me. He was always helping me out whenever I had one of my projects. I wouldn't even have to ask. As soon as he saw me working, he'd come running. And most of the time, you would be trailing right there behind him. He was so damn proud of you. Always bragging on something you'd done. Used to say you had the heart of a lion, and you felt the same way about him. You two were inseparable." He took a drag off of his cigarette and continued. "When he died, it was difficult for all of us, but you took it the hardest. It took some time, but eventually, you learned to live with your loss. You were there for your mother and brother, taking his place the best way you knew how. I tried my hardest to take up the slack when I could, but I knew it wasn't the same."

"You've always been there for us, Bishop. But this... covering up what I did? I can't ask you to do that."

"It's already done. You may not be my blood, Sunny, but you are my family just the same. I look after my own, and I intend to keep doing that until the day I take my last breath."

His words settled in her heart, giving her a sense of peace that she desperately needed. As always, he was there. She'd always known he was a good man, just like her father, but the realization of everything he'd done and why made her love him even more. "I don't know how I will ever repay you."

"You already have. You survived. That's all I needed in return," Bishop smiled.

Sunny turned and leaned against the rails as she looked out at the pond. "I don't know how I'm supposed to move on from all of this. How do I just forget that I killed someone?"

"Back when Myles was trying out for basketball, I remember you trying to help him work on his rebound. He took a pretty nasty fall and banged up his knee. He was all scratched up and bleeding, and he was about to have a complete meltdown. But you walked over and knelt down beside him and whispered something in his ear. A few seconds later, he pulled himself off the ground and shook off the dirt from his shorts. He was slow moving, but he took the ball from your hand and took his shot. It wasn't long before he'd forgotten that he'd ever taken the fall."

"There's no telling what I said to him," Sunny

laughed.

"I asked him later what you'd said." Bishop walked over next to her and placed his hand on her shoulder. "You told him, it's not the fall that defines you, but the shots you make once you get up. So, Sunny... I'd say it's time for you to pick yourself up and take your shot."

Chapter 14

The sun was just starting to set over the lake as Sunny sat on the dock watching the boats putter in and out of the bay. It was a place her father had taken her when she was little. They watched as the different boats passed by and took turns telling stories about the people that were tucked away inside, each tale more elaborate than the last. As a large yacht pulled into the dock, she tried to imagine what her father might say about the family onboard. Maybe he'd tell her that they'd been traveling for months and had just come home for Christmas, or that they planned to spend time with their family and friends before they headed off to Paris for the spring. She missed her father, and now more than ever, she needed him to be there. She longed to feel his strong arms wrapped around her, protecting her from all the chaos that was whirling around her. Most of all, she needed to hear the comforting sound of his voice telling her that everything would be okay, that like all the people in his stories, she too would find her happy ending.

Just as darkness fell around her, little white Christmas lights flickered on, illuminating the entire dock. It was beautiful, but the night air grew colder, making her body tremble beneath her coat. She knew it was long past time for her to go. After all, it was Christmas Eve. Everyone would be heading over to Bishop's, and she knew they would be expecting her to be there. She didn't want to let them down. They'd all been so patient with her, especially Gavin. Over the past few weeks, he'd been there to listen when she cried, to hold her when she felt lost, and to reassure her when she was overcome with doubts. He was her strength and he never failed to be there when she needed him. Now was no different. She was staring out at the lake, watching the lights dance along the water. When she heard her phone buzz with a text message, she looked down at the screen and saw that it was Gavin. Just seeing his name made her lips curl into a smile.

Gavin:

Hey. You up for some company?

Sunny:

Sorry. I'm not at home.

Gavin:

I know you're not. That wasn't my question.

Sunny:

I'm always up for your company.

The Long Road Home

Gavin:

Good. I was hoping you'd say that.

Seconds later, he strolled up the walkway and sat down on the bench beside her. When he saw her red nose and cheeks, he took off his coat and wrapped it around her. "How long have you been out here?"

"A while."

"Everything okay?"

"It is now." She smiled as she nestled into the crook of his arm. "I'm glad you came."

"It's been a long day and I was ready to see my girl." He put his arm around her and pulled her close. "You about ready to head over to Bishop's?"

"I guess so."

"Good. I hope you aren't planning to stay too long. I've got plans for you later."

"Plans? What kind of plans?"

"The kind of plan where you are in my bed screaming out my name when the man in red comes flying overhead."

She laughed as she stood up. "Sounds like a good plan to me."

"Then let's get moving. You ride with me. I'll get one of the guys to bring your car over to the apartment later."

"Okay."

She followed him over to his Jeep and just before

she got inside, he handed her a white box and said, "I've got something for you."

"What is this?"

"Open it and see."

She'd heard stories about the white box from the girls when they shared their stories about becoming ol' ladies, and she couldn't help but wonder if her time had finally come to receive her cut. She carefully opened the box and peeked inside. A smile spread across her face when she saw the familiar Devil Chaser's patch. She quickly pulled the leather jacket out of the box and put it on. "Is this for real?"

"As real as it gets." He put his hands on her hips and pulled her over to him. "After you graduate, I'll put a ring on your finger and we'll make it official in every way."

"I love you, Gavin."

"And I love you." He pressed his lips against hers, kissing her with all the love and passion he had to give. He knew in that moment, he had everything he'd ever wanted.

Their kiss led to more than he'd expected, and they were late getting to Bishop's. By the time they'd arrived, everyone was already sitting down at the table. Sunny tried to slip in unnoticed, but as soon as Courtney caught sight of her new jacket, she shouted, "Well, lookie here! We've got ourselves another Old Lady!"

All eyes were quickly drawn over to Sunny, making

her face bright red as they all started to hoot and holler. Sheppard smiled as he said, "It's about damn time."

Tessa stood up and walked over to her, giving her a hug. "Congratulations, sweetie. You got yourself a good one."

"Thanks, Tess. I think he's pretty wonderful."

"He sure loves you. There's no doubt about that."

Once all the girls had taken their turn congratulating Sunny, Gavin reached for her hand and led her over to the table. After they'd gotten settled, Bishop raised his glass and said, "To new beginnings!"

Everyone followed suit and lifted their glasses as they repeated, "To new beginnings."

Sunny looked over to her mother and placed her hand on her arm. "Merry Christmas, Momma."

Glenda leaned towards her, hugging her tightly as she said, "Merry Christmas, sweetheart. It's good to see you looking so happy."

"I am happy, Momma. Very happy."

She looked up at her daughter, seeing the bright smile on her face, and the anxiousness she'd been carrying around with her for weeks finally started to fade. Seeing her now, she knew in her heart that her daughter was going to be okay, that the hell they'd been through was finally over. She gave her another quick squeeze before she said, "That's all I've ever wanted."

"Love you, Mom."

"I love you, too, sweetheart. Now, finish your

dinner. I brought something special for dessert tonight."

Gavin leaned forward and looked over to Glenda as he asked, "Dessert?"

"It's a surprise." Glenda smiled.

"Oh, man. You're killing me, Ms. Glenda."

"Trust me, it will be worth the wait." She chuckled and then turned her attention back to her dinner. She nudged Sunny's side with her elbow as she whispered, "He's a keeper."

"That he is."

It was just after midnight when Sunny and Gavin got back to her apartment. Katelyn had gone to stay the night with her folks, so they had the place to themselves. After changing into one of her t-shirts, Sunny turned on the Christmas tree and put in a silly Christmas movie. She pulled her fleece blanket over her bare legs as she got settled on the sofa. Before joining her, Gavin reached behind the tree and pulled out a small red box. With a hopeful look in his eye, he took it over and placed it in Sunny's hand. "Open it."

She studied the small rectangular box, turning it back and forth in her hand. He'd already given her everything she wanted, and she couldn't imagine what was inside. She carefully eased the box open and found plane tickets tucked inside. She quickly pulled them out and shouted, "We're going to Barbados?"

"Thought I'd take you during your spring break. Spend some time acting like a couple of crazy college kids."

She reached over and gave him an excited hug, then looked back down at the tickets. "I can't believe we're going to Jamaica to spend a week at the beach!"

"Well, we are, and that's just the start."

She stared at them for several more seconds before she hopped off the sofa and rushed over to the Christmas tree, reaching for her gift for Gavin. She grabbed the large, heavy box and lugged it back over to him. "Your turn."

His eyebrows furrowed as he looked down at the package. He hadn't seen it under the tree and wondered when she'd gotten it. He pulled the paper back and opened the box, finding a new set of lower fairings for his bike. He'd been looking at the exact set online for weeks, but kept talking himself out of buying them. "This is too much."

"No, it's not." She sat down next to him and continued, "I knew you'd been wanting them, and it will help keep you a little warmer when it's cold."

"You didn't have to do that, but thank you." He placed the box on the table, then leaned towards her, forcing her back against the sofa cushions. His mouth dropped as he began to nip and suck along the curve of her neck.

"I take it you like them?" she giggled.

"Love 'em, but I'm ready for my next Christmas present." He settled himself on the floor between her legs, then reached for the waistband of her pink lace panties and eased them down her legs. "Been thinking about having you like this since I saw you sitting out there by the dock."

He pulled his shirt over his head, then lowered his mouth down between her legs. She gasped and arched her back when his tongue skimmed across her clit. He teased back and forth in a gentle rhythm against her sensitive flesh, loving the way her body instantly reacted to his touch. Her fingers delved into his hair, gripping him tightly as her hips squirmed below him. Her breath became ragged and short when he thrusted his finger deep inside her, twirling against her G-spot with a slow and steady pace. While he continued to tease her clit with his tongue, he added a second finger, driving deeper and sliding farther inside her. She tensed around him as her body rocked against his hand. Seeing the goosebumps prickling across her skin and knowing he was getting to her, he smiled against her flesh, loving the effect he was having on her. He continued to nip and suck the inside of her thigh as her hips lifted up from the sofa, begging for him to give her more. He drove his fingers deeper inside her, caressing her delicate flesh. Her body shuddered as she released his hair, dropping her hands to the cushions of the sofa and digging into the fabric as she started to tremble uncontrollably.

"Oh god, Gavin," she panted.

He continued to tease that spot that was driving her

to the edge as his tongue teased her clit. She murmured his name over and over as she clenched around his fingers. She was still in the throes of her release as he dropped his jeans to the floor. After slipping on a condom, he settled between her legs and pulled her over to the edge of the sofa. He looked down at her, thinking how fucking beautiful she looked, and his entire body ached with need. He hovered over her, brushing his cock across her entrance. She didn't move; she laid there, legs spread, just begging to be taken, and he couldn't imagine wanting anything more. With a wicked grin, she shifted her hips, forcing him inside her. Unable to resist, he thrust deeply.

"You never stop amazing me," he whispered in her ear as he slid her t-shirt up over her stomach, revealing her perfect round breasts. He took her nipple in his mouth and felt her breath quicken as his teeth raked across her flesh.

"Yes," she moaned, her legs instinctively wrapping around his waist as she pulled him deeper inside her. He slowly withdrew, then gradually eased back inside her. His pace was steady and unforgiving. His eyes roamed over her, taking in every inch of her gorgeous body. Her chest rose and fell as she tried to steady her breath, each gasp of air sounding more desperate than the last. Shifting her hips upward, she ground her hips against him, urging him to give her more. His pace never faltered as he continued to thrust inside her, over and over, constantly increasing the rhythm of his movements.

"Fuck!" he shouted out as his throbbing cock demanded its release too soon. He wanted to take his time with her–savor every moment–but she felt too fucking good to stop. He plunged inside of her again and again, feeling her spasm with her release. His hips collided into hers, his thrusts coming faster and harder with every breath he took.

He gazed down at her, in awe of her strength and how she'd overcome so much. He was amazed that she was his. He loved her, body and soul, and there was nothing he wouldn't do for her. She was his heart, his home, his everything.

She jolted as her orgasm riveted through her body. Hearing the light whimpers of his name echoing through the room sent him over the edge, and he couldn't hold back any longer, giving in to his own release.

A sexy, satisfied grin crossed her face as Sunny looked up at him and said, "I'd say the man in red got an earful tonight."

"I reckon he did," Gavin chuckled. He eased himself off the sofa and pulled her into his arms, cradling her as he carried her into the bedroom. After tossing the covers back, he lowered her onto the bed and slid in beside her. She nestled up close to him, resting her head on his shoulder, and they lay there in the dark, listening to the sound of the rain thumping against the roof. He pressed his lips against her temple and said, "Merry Christmas, Lucky."

"Merry Christmas, Gavin."

Two years later.

"Gavin. Can you come here for a second?" Sunny called as she waited in the bathroom for him to answer.

"Be right there." After what seemed to be an eternity, Gavin appeared before her wearing a short sleeve t-shirt and a pair of clean jeans.

With her eyebrow raised high, she looked at him with his freshly-washed clothes and sighed with frustration. Using her best dramatic display, she motioned her hand over to the mountain of dirty clothes that were sprawled across the floor. "What is this?"

He leaned to the side, looking behind her as he answered, "What?"

"That!"

"What?"

"The dirty clothes on the floor."

"Well, how about that. Looks like you already know what they are," he chuckled.

Not long after Sunny graduated, Gavin bought them a house out by the lake. He'd wanted to do it sooner, but he'd made a promise to Sunny's mother and himself that he wouldn't become a distraction to Sunny. As much as he wanted to be with her night and day, he was patient and waited for her to get her degree before they moved in together. Thankfully, with the hours she'd already accumulated and the classes she took in summer school, she'd managed to graduate sooner than they'd expected. Soon after, they moved in together. They'd only been living in the new house for a few months, and Sunny was learning the hard way that living with a man wasn't always easy. But, there was one thing about Sunny: she was determined.

"Okay… let's try this." With a scolding look, she pointed to the corner. "What is that thing sitting beside the pile of dirty clothes on the floor?"

He rested his hip against the sink and crossed his arms. "That'd be the laundry basket."

She threw her hands up in the air and sassed, "Praise God! He does know what it is!"

"You got a point to all this, Lucky?"

"I do," she said sarcastically as she walked over to the pile of dirty clothes. She took a handful and tossed them into the laundry basket. "The dirty clothes go in the *laundry basket*."

"Mm-hmm," he smirked.

"Dirty clothes. *Laundry Basket*. You think you can handle that?"

"You're cute when you get all worked up, you know that?" he said as he took a step towards her. He knew she was trying to be serious, but he just couldn't stop himself. Seeing her with her hand propped on her hip and that spark in her eye made it impossible for him to resist.

Seeing the look in his eyes, she shook her head and said, "Oh, no you don't. I know that look." She took a step back and pointed her finger at him. "Getting me all hot and bothered isn't gonna make those dirty clothes magically disappear."

"Maybe I like getting you all hot and bothered," he teased as he took another step towards her.

"Gavin. *Focus.*"

"Oh, I'm *focused.*" He pulled his t-shirt over his head and tossed it into the laundry basket. Sounding overly cocky, he told her, "See? I can handle it. Dirty clothes in the laundry basket."

Her eyes dropped to his bare chest and she had to fight the urge to pounce on him like a horny teenager. Trying her best to ignore her raging hormones, she turned away from him and said, "Good. That's all I'm asking."

"What about the toothpaste situation?"

"What toothpaste *situation*?"

He reached for the toothpaste and held up the dented tube as he said, "Didn't your momma teach you to squeeze from the bottom?"

"Seriously?"

"And there's a cap for a reason," he mocked, knowing that he was hitting all of her buttons. He dropped the toothpaste on the counter and looked back over to her as he said, "And while we're at it... we should probably discuss the cat."

"What about the cat?"

"You know the toilet isn't exactly the best place for her to get her water. You might try giving her some fresh water from time to time."

Aggravation crossed her face as she took a step towards him. "I give her fresh water every day! It's not my fault she's crazy, and she wouldn't do it if you'd just put down the seat."

"Umm-hmmm." He could care less about the tooth paste or where the cat got her water; he was trying to get under her skin and it was working. He had to think for a second to find anything else he could throw at her. "And what about the *Doritos*?"

"Oh my heavens. What about the *Doritos*?"

"You know they're my favorite, but you keep finishing off the bag before I can get to them."

"Okay. I'll leave your Doritos alone from now on," she huffed.

"I'd appreciate that." He reached into his pocket, pulling out a small black box, and took a step towards her. "Well, now that we've got that settled... what about this?"

Sunny gasped as she looked at the gorgeous, diamond engagement ring. Before she could register what was happening, he dropped down on one knee and said, "Things in my life haven't always been easy. There were times when I lost my way and thought I would never get to the good. I thought my mistakes were holding me back, but the entire time they were leading me home… They were leading me to you." He took the ring out of the box and reached for her hand, slipping it onto her finger. "I've never been happier. Will you give me the chance to make you as happy as you've made me? Sunny, will you marry me?"

Sunny lunged forward, wrapping her arms around his neck as she shrieked, "Yes! Yes, I will marry you!!'

He held her close to his chest, hugging her tightly as he stood up. Even though he knew in his heart she'd say yes, hearing the words aloud made it feel so surreal. With her, his life made sense. She grounded him and made him look to the future instead of being consumed by the past, and he did the same for her. Together, they were better. It was as simple as that.

"When?"

She looked up at him. "I don't know. When do you want to do it?"

"The sooner, the better." He pressed his lips to hers, kissing her tenderly. "I'll do whatever you want, just don't make me wait too long."

"I'll do my best." She looked down at the ring on her finger. "I can't believe we just got engaged in our bathroom. That's going to be a story. Courtney is going to have a field day with this one."

"Wanted to take you by surprise."

"Well, you definitely did that." She smiled as she

wound her arms around his neck. "I love you so much. Thank you, Gavin."

"For what?"

"For giving me my happy ending."

The End.

More to come from the Devil Chaser's Series in the late summer or early fall.

Author's Note

I had some readers ask about the recipes that were mentioned in the book. If you haven't had a chance to try Chess pie or you want to know about the cream cheese do-doobers, I am including links to their recipes. These are some of my favorite Christmas time treats:

Chess Pie:

http://allrecipes.com/recipe/9090/chess-pie/

Cream Cheese Squares:

http://www.myrecipes.com/recipe/cheesecake-crescent-rolls

Cherry Delight:

http://allrecipes.com/recipe/231310/opals-cherry-delight/

Acknowledgements

Amanda Faulkner – There are no words to express how much your help means to me. You never fail to be there when I need you, and your dedication astounds me. Thank you for all you do. Love you big!

Natalie Weston – You are such a great voice of reason. Thank you for being there to keep me level headed and pointed in the right direction. You are awesome.

Daryl and Sue Banner, The Dynamic Duo – Thank you both for making my books the best they can be. I don't know what I'd do without you. Love you both! Daryl isn't just an editor. He's also an amazing author. If you haven't checked out his books, you are missing out. They are amazing!!

https://www.amazon.com/author/darylbanner

Lisa Cullinan – Thank you so very much for always being there and going the extra mile. You a such a blessing, and I am so very thankful to have you. I told Santa to be extra good to you this year!!

Neringa Neringiukas – You are the teaser guru.

Thank you so much for sharing my book and teasers, and all of your kind words of support. You rock!

Danielle Deraney Palumbo – Thank you! You are such a blessing to me, and your help always means so much. I truly appreciate you!

Kaci Stewart, Tanya Skaggs, Lisa Cullinan, Terra Oenning, Jamie Richards Morgan, Jordan Marie, Beth Alarcon, Rachel Hadley, Demetra Toula Illiopoulos, Stacie Page-Ramay, and Patricia Ann Bevins – Thank you so much for always being there with your kind words and support. You ladies are awesome.

Wilder's Women – I am always amazed at how much you do to help promote my books with your reviews and all of your posts. Thank you for being a part of this journey with me.

A Special Thanks to Mom – Thank you for always being there to read, chapter by chapter, giving me your complete support. I love you so very much, and it means the world to me that you that you love my characters as much as I do.

77187807R00113

Made in the USA
San Bernardino, CA
20 May 2018